Mr. Plakcy did a terrific job in this cozy mystery. He had a smooth writing style that kept the story flowing evenly. The dialogue and descriptions were right on target.

Red Adept

Steve and Rochester become quite a team and Neil Plakcy is the kind of writer that I want to tell me this story. It's a fun read which will keep you turning pages very quickly.

Amos Lassen – Amazon top 100 reviewer

In Dog We Trust is a very well-crafted mystery that kept me guessing up until Steve figured out where things were going.

E-book addict reviews

Neil Plakcy's *Kingdom of Dog* is supposed to be about the former computer hacker, now college professor, Steve Levitan, but it is his golden retriever Rochester who is the real amateur sleuth in this delightful academic mystery. This is no talking dog book, though. Rochester doesn't need anything more than his wagging tail and doggy smile to win over readers and help solve crimes. I absolutely fell in love with this brilliant dog who digs up clues and points the silly humans towards the evidence.

Christine Kling, author of *Circle of Bones*

A Litter of Golden Mysteries

Neil S. Plakcy

Samwise Books
www.mahubooks.com

This cozy mystery is a work of fiction. Names, characters, places, and incidents either are products of the author's imagination or are used fictitiously. Any resemblance to actual events or locales or persons, living or dead, is entirely coincidental.

All rights reserved, including the right of reproduction in whole or in part in any form.

Copyright 2020 by Neil S. Plakcy

Published by Samwise Books

Cover art by: Kelly Nichols
Formatting by Kris Jacen

Issued 2020

This book is licensed to the original purchaser only. Duplication or distribution via any means is illegal and a violation of International Copyright Law, subject to criminal prosecution and upon conviction, fines and/or imprisonment. This eBook cannot be legally loaned or given to others. No part of this eBook can be shared or reproduced without the express permission of the publisher

A few of the titles were previously published.

"Dog Forbid" originally appeared in *Happy Homicides, Volume 1*. Spot On Publishing, 2015.

"For the Love of Dog" originally appeared in *Happy Homicides 2: Crimes of the Heart*. Spot On Publishing, 2016.

"Riding the Tiger" originally appeared in *Happy Homicides, Volume 5: The Purr-fect Crime*. Spot On Publishing, 2017.

"Nectar of the Dogs" originally appeared in *Happy Homicides, Volume 6: Cookin' Up Crime*. Spot On Publishing, 2017.

"Crime Dog on the Road" and "Doggy DNA" were recorded by Thomas Nance and featured on the MysteryRat's podcast sponsored by King's River Life magazine.

Contents

Story 1: Dog Works in Mysterious Ways 1

Story 2: Dog Forbid 19

    Part 1 – Holiday Plans 19

    Part 2 – Dog-Friendly 24

    Part 3 – Van Makes an Entrance 29

    Part 4 – Slipped Away 34

    Part 5 – Action Plans 37

    Part 6 – Companion Puppy 39

    Part 7 – A Smart Boy 42

Story 3: Riding the Tiger 53

Story 4: Crime Dog on the Road 77

Story 5: For the Love of Dog 83

    Part 1 – As White as Flour 83

    Part 2 – Hardy Boys 88

    Part 3 – Angry Brush Strokes 93

    Part 4 – Crossed Wires 99

  Part 5 – Ethnic Fix 105

  Part 6 – Carpe Diem Moment 111

  Part 7 – The Four Types of Love 115

  Part 8 – Valentine's Day 122

Story 6: Nectar of the Dogs 125

Story 7: Dog's Only Son 141

Story 8: Doggy DNA 151

Story 9: Walking the Dog: A Story in Text Messages 155

Story 1: Dog Works in Mysterious Ways

At two years old, my golden retriever Rochester was still a big puppy, with a habit of sticking his wet black nose where it didn't belong. When I heard something fall downstairs, I hurried to the staircase. From the landing, I saw him scratching his paw against the packing tape on one of the boxes stacked along the living room wall.

The row of identical cardboard boxes had been there since I moved in. While I was serving a brief prison term in California for computer hacking, my father passed away, leaving me a townhouse in my hometown of Stewart's Crossing, Pennsylvania in his will. At the time, I thought I was going to sell the place, so I hired a company to clean and pack up.

My marriage also fell apart while I was in prison, so I returned to Bucks County with my tail metaphorically between my legs, trying to start over. I'd been in the house for over a year and I still hadn't unpacked the boxes of my dad's stuff.

Maybe Rochester thought he was giving me a kick start. By the time I grabbed him by the collar and pulled him away, he had detached a strip of tape and one side of the box had popped open.

"I don't have time for this now," I said, reaching down to press the box closed again. "Lili's going to be here any minute."

But a strip of buttery light-brown suede caught my eye, and I opened the box instead of resealing it. The item on top was a sports jacket, softened from wear, that my father had often worn on cool fall afternoons when he, my mother and I prowled the flea market in search of bargains.

I tried it on, and it fit perfectly. The lining was torn and a button was missing, but that could all be fixed. Rochester sat on his haunches watching me, and I wondered if it was the smell of the leather that had attracted him to that box.

Suddenly he jumped up and skittered across the tile floor to the front door, and he was there by the time my girlfriend Lili opened it.

It seemed strange to use the word 'girlfriend' to describe our relationship, when we were both over forty, but the English language had not caught up to modern life. In Lili's case, though, the term worked, because she had an enthusiasm for the world that was almost girlish, despite the years she had spent as a photojournalist covering danger spots.

"Hi, Steve. Nice jacket," she said. "New?"

We met halfway to the door and kissed. "Nope, it belonged to my dad. Rochester decided it was time for me to start unpacking the boxes he left behind."

"Rochester has good instincts. Don't you boy?" She handed me the large sealed plastic container she was carrying and reached down to pet the dog's silky head.

I lifted one corner of the container and sniffed. "Smells delicious. Lemon chicken. Capers, too?"

She and Rochester followed me to the kitchen. "Just something I threw together. You still have that bottle of prosecco? Why don't you pour while I put the food out."

"Sure." I opened the bottle as she took the chicken out and put it on a platter. Rochester nosed around us in the kitchen, eager to sample our dinner. "You said you had some big news. What's up?"

"Let me finish this," she said. "I'll tell you once we sit down to eat."

She was a tall woman, a couple of inches shorter than my six-one, with an exuberant mass of auburn curls held in tenuous place by a series of brightly colored barrettes. She wore a pair of black slacks and a tan long-sleeved man-tailored shirt. "You're losing a butterfly," I said, picking off a yellow-and-brown barrette just before it fell into the chicken. "I don't think it would add much to the flavor."

She took the clip from me and replaced it. "Probably not."

She carried the platter out to the table in the breakfast nook, where I'd already set the table, and I followed her with the wine. She sat down across from me, and Rochester snuggled up against her chair hoping for a handout.

"So, *nu*?" I asked, reverting to the Yiddish expression I'd heard thousands of times as a kid, as I helped myself to the redolent chicken.

She took a deep breath. "Van called me this morning. He's about to head out to Albania to report on another cruise ship problem, and his photographer came down with dysentery."

"Van? Van Dryver? Your ex-boyfriend?"

"I told you, Steve, he wasn't really a boyfriend. We had a fling, a hundred years ago. Now we're just colleagues."

"How are you colleagues? You're a professor and he's a reporter."

"In this case he's a reporter and I'm a photojournalist. He asked me to come with him and take pictures, and I said yes."

"But what about your job?" Lili was the chair of the fine arts department at Eastern College, where I handled press relations for the college's fund-raising campaign.

"The trip is just for a week or two." She frowned at me like I was a student who wasn't getting the point. "Van called me this morning. A cruise ship on its way to Corfu broke down in the Strait of Otranto late last night. There are a lot of questions about what it was doing so close to the Albanian coast, and Van heard a rumor some sophisticated electronics on board might be part of a spy operation. He got an assignment from the *Wall Street Journal* for a business story about the rash of problems with cruise ships lately—but he's hoping there's something more."

"Okay, I get that part. But why you?"

"What do you mean, why me? I used to do this for a living, you know."

I waved my hand. "I don't mean that. But there are a lot of photographers he could call. Why you?"

"Van and I used to talk about bucket lists a lot," she said. "Places we wanted to go before we died. Albania was on both our lists. He remembered, so when this other guy got sick he thought of me."

"Are you sure he's not trying to get back together with you?"

"Oh, you're jealous. That's sweet. But I outgrew Van a long time ago. This is just business." She waved at the meal. "Eat."

As we ate, I made appreciative noises about the food, but my mind was going in a hundred different directions. Should I be jealous of Van? Worried about Lili heading to what might be a dangerous assignment? She didn't need my permission, but she hadn't even asked for my opinion before deciding to go, and that bothered me.

Finally, Lili put down her knife and fork and looked at me across the table. "There's something else I want to talk to you about," she said.

I waited as she scooped up the last piece of chicken and fed it to Rochester, who wolfed it down greedily.

Then she nodded toward the stack of boxes. "Sometimes, when I'm here, I feel like there's no space for me. We've both been keeping each other at a distance, because of our past, but I feel like I'm moving forward and you aren't. You need to come to terms with everything that's holding you back."

I was blindsided. Not just by the announcement that Lili was taking off with her ex-fling, but by her comment about our future, too. Sure, I knew I had to get around to unpacking those boxes someday, but I hadn't felt any urgency. And Lili had never complained about them before.

I felt that she was expecting a response from me, but I didn't have one. After she waited a couple of beats, she stood up to clear the table. "I packed before I left my apartment, and I have everything I need in my trunk. Do you think you could drive me to the airport in Philly tonight, and I could leave my car here?"

"Tonight?" My voice squeaked. "So soon?"

"It's news," she said. "Kind of requires immediate action."

I stood up, too. I was determined to be adult about this, even if I didn't want to be. "Sure. What time?"

"I'm booked on a red-eye to Rome at eleven. Tomorrow morning I'll meet up with Van and we'll fly into Tirana. He'll have all the visas by then."

"And if not? You guys will just hang out in Rome together?"

"I'll be fine, and you don't have to worry about me falling for Van again. All right?" She stepped over to me and kissed me. "I know this may seem like it's coming out of the blue, but I've been thinking about our future together, and this trip with Van is pushing everything forward."

"I understand. And I appreciate what you're saying." Rochester tried to nose his way between us. "Even the dog agrees, I guess."

"Good. We have time for one long walk before I go, if you both want to."

"Rochester's always ready for a walk." I smiled at Lili. "And I'm always happy to spend time with you."

As we strolled down Sarajevo Court in the golden light of early evening, I thought about Lili's comment, that I needed to deal with my past. It was a complicated one, for sure, though I thought I'd been managing well enough.

Once upon a time, I was a computer executive, married to a beautiful, successful woman. We lived in Silicon Valley and we were trying to have a child. After Mary suffered two miscarriages, though, everything fell apart and I ended up in prison.

Since then, I had restarted my career, first as an adjunct professor at Eastern, then as an administrator. Rochester had become my surrogate child, and his love had helped me open my heart to Lili. What else did I have to do to deal with my past? Unpack a few boxes?

We walked slowly past mature trees and townhouses with a vague Eastern European air, from the gabled roofs to the stone fronts, arches and fake bell towers on the end units. Lili would soon be in the part of the world where this architecture had originated, I thought, and I'd be back here. But we'd both have work to do.

Rochester pranced ahead of us, his golden plume of a tail held high and proud. Suddenly he stopped and lowered his head, pointing his snout forward.

I knew what that meant. "No squirrels!" I said, yanking on his leash just as he lunged forward.

The little rodent scampered up the trunk of an oak, and Rochester jumped up and placed his paws on the bark. An acorn dropped from above and hit him squarely on the snout. He yelped and backed down.

"That'll teach you," I said, laughing.

Lili reached up to brush away a curl. "Oh, crap," she said. "I lost that barrette, the one that was loose. I knew I should have just put it away."

"Rochester is ready to turn around and head for home," I said. "We can look for it on the way."

I leaned down to the shaggy dog. "You hear that, boy? Lili lost her barrette. You're going to find it for us, right?"

He shook his head but I couldn't tell if that was a yes or a no. All the way back we scanned the street and the lawns, looking for one of her yellow-and-brown butterflies, but with no success. "It's all right," Lili said. "I can rearrange the ones I have on my head. But I am bummed. I bought them from an artisan's shop in a small town in Eritrea. I know I'm never going back there."

"I'll look again tomorrow morning. While I'm thinking of you landing in Rome."

When we got back to the house, I shifted her big backpack from her trunk to mine. It was surprisingly light, and I remarked on it. "Have to be able to get on the road quickly if the story moves," she said.

Rochester scrambled into the back seat, and I drove Lili to the airport. She spent most of the trip on her phone, either pecking out emails or confirming details with a dozen different people, from the assignment editor at the *Journal* to a doctor's office where she left a message to reschedule an appointment.

I stopped in the departure lane, and she kissed me goodbye, then walked off with her backpack and her camera bag without a backward glance. Rochester moved up front as I inched my way out of the airport and then got back on the highway.

Her trip worried me. I didn't trust Van, her ex-boyfriend, and I worried that if he uncovered some nefarious deeds connected with the fire on the cruise ship, he'd be putting himself and Lili in danger.

When we got home, I looked for information online about the incident Lili and Van were investigating. The Siren had been on a cruise from Venice to Athens, making stops in several picturesque towns along the Croatian coast. It broke down near a rocky, nearly unoccupied peninsula that stuck out into the Ionian Sea as if Albania was giving the finger to its neighbors. The Albanian Defense Force had taken control of the ship and directed it to dock in Durrës, a cruise port due west of the capital.

That was all I could find. The next morning, Saturday, I signed up for a free trial of the *Journal's* web content, and searched for Van's byline. He hadn't posted anything yet; but then, he and Lili hadn't reached Albania by then.

After a quick breakfast, I stood in my living room and looked at Rochester. "What do you think, boy? Should I do some unpacking?"

He didn't say anything, just walked over to the row of boxes and slumped to the floor. The box that had contained my dad's suede jacket was still open, so I started there. Beneath it I found cards and letters I had sent home from overseas trips, a composite picture of my third-grade class, and a set of Isaac Asimov's *Foundation* trilogy. It was all so random, and that made it a process of discovery.

I used the Swiss Army Knife my father had given me for my sixteenth birthday to slice open the next box, where the newspaper packing was dated soon after my mother passed away. The careful way the box had been packed told me right away it had been done by my father.

As I sliced the tape around the first item, I wondered what he had thought was worth saving. I unfolded the paper to reveal a small pale green Lenox china bird, no gold details or other ornamentation. It was about three inches tall, with its face turned upward.

I remembered that bird. My father had bought it for my mother for their first anniversary, knowing how much she loved Lenox, which was manufactured in Trenton, New Jersey, the city where both she and I had been born. I carried it to the china cabinet and set it in the front.

As I continued to unpack, I found more mementoes of my parents' lives together. When they were first married, he worked as an engineering temp for different companies, a few months at a time. When he returned from each out-of-town assignment, he brought her an antique perfume bottle—crystal, porcelain, cloisonné, each one different.

It seemed like everything my father packed away was something connected to the two of them. None of the paperback romances she loved to read, or items she had bought for herself. It was almost as if he was preparing for me this record of a happy marriage, even as my own was falling apart.

After unpacking for a couple of hours, I was beginning to drown in my family's past. To clear my head, I took Rochester for a long walk, out of River Bend and down toward the Delaware Canal, which ran behind downtown Stewart's Crossing. In the summer the towpath beside the canal was lined with the tiny pansies we called Johnny Jump-Ups, patches of black-eyed Susans, and other wildflowers. It was a great place to let Rochester off his leash for a good run.

I sat on the grassy bank of the canal. Rochester darted back and forth behind me for a minute, then took off down the canal. "Don't go too far," I called. Then I relaxed and stared up above at the puffy clouds floating across the light-blue sky.

I thought about my parents' lives, and their marriage. They had always squabbled, but insisted that it was just their way of communicating. And the relics my father had saved testified to the love between them.

Rochester finally ran out of steam, and collapsed beside me. I stroked his head, and remembered that after my mother's death, I'd worried about my dad, back home alone in Stewart's Crossing. When he announced he was selling the house where I grew up to buy the townhouse in River Bend, I hoped that meant he was getting along. He mentioned occasional dinners out with various elderly women, trips to the racetrack with old friends. But I was too caught up in my own troubles to do much for him.

We walked back home soon after that, and I checked my laptop for newer reports on the Siren, but there was little to find. By my calculations Lili had been in Rome for a few hours, and might have already left for Tirana, the Albanian capital—providing Van was able to secure the necessary visas. Why hadn't Lili emailed me yet? Surely she'd been able to get Wi-Fi access somewhere?

My heart skipped a beat when my laptop pinged with the notice of an incoming email from Lili. She had sent a snapshot of an airplane and the note that she was boarding it for Albania.

Each time I took Rochester outside to walk, and saw Lili's car parked beside mine, I thought of her, and what she had said before she left. Sunday morning, I fed and walked the dog, then continued to unpack. By the time I'd finished the third box, though, I was once again overwhelmed with emotion. Each new item brought back memories of my parents and my childhood—a giant clamshell, souvenir of a Jersey shore vacation. My bar mitzvah certificate. A hand-carved figurine of a duck that had sat on my dad's workbench. An old prayer book, all in Hebrew, that had been in my family for generations.

I don't know when I started crying, or why. Was it the long-forgotten memories? Or was I finally reconciling myself to my father's loss, especially as I hadn't been able to attend his funeral? Rochester came over to where I sat on the tile floor of the living room and snuffled me, and I reached out to stroke his flank as he settled against me.

Once when I was a teenager, my father and I were watching a TV program about Jewish immigration, and a man mentioned that even though he had left his family behind in Europe, when his father died, he had said the Kaddish, the ritual prayer recited at funerals, grave sites and during memorials for the dead.

My father had turned to me then and said, "I expect you to say Kaddish for me." I could still hear his voice in my head and remember staring at him in confusion. I was a teenager, and my parents seemed immortal then. I couldn't imagine then the losses I would face in the future.

I picked up the prayer book and flipped it open, looking for the Kaddish prayer, scanning the Hebrew letters, looking for a familiar pattern. I can't carry on a conversation in the language, but I did spend three years of weekday afternoons in Hebrew school and I could still make out the letters.

When I found it, for the first time I looked at the English translation. I had always thought the prayer was about loss, confusing it with the 23rd Psalm and its walk through the valley of the shadow of death. But instead, it was a paean to God's glory, and the only hint of sorrow came in the last line: "He who creates peace in His celestial heights, may He create peace for us and for all Israel; and say, Amen."

Wasn't peace, after all, what mourners sought? A reconciliation to loss and a recognition that God, in his wisdom and greatness, was responsible for birth and death.

I began to recite the Hebrew, part from memory and part from deciphering the letters on the page, stroking Rochester's side as I did. When I came to the end, I looked down at him and smiled, and said those last words to him in the language of my ancestors, a people who were very familiar with suffering and loss. "*O-seh shalom bim romav, hu ya-aseh shalom aleinu v'al kol Yisroel, v'imru* Amen."

§ § §

About noon, I heard a vehicle pull up in front of my house, and I walked to the front door. My friend Rick Stemper was standing by his truck, with his Australian shepherd Rascal in the back.

"I'm going to take Rascal for a run," Rick said. "You guys want to come? Or are you doing something with Lili?"

Rochester pushed past me to the courtyard gate and began barking madly when he spotted his friend. Rascal returned the barks.

"I'll be right out," I called, over the cacophony. I locked up the house and let Rochester run down the driveway to Rick's truck. Rick opened the tailgate and Rochester launched himself at Rascal, and the two of them began to romp.

"Lili left Friday night for Albania," I said, as Rick closed the tailgate. "With her ex-boyfriend."

He cocked his head to the side in a gesture that reminded me of Rochester. "Excuse me?"

We got into the truck and he began to drive. "This guy Van is an investigative reporter for the *Wall Street Journal*," I said. "He was getting ready to head to Albania to report on that cruise ship fire and his photographer got sick. So he asked Lili."

"Convenient for him, huh?"

"Yeah. I mean, I know he's a jerk, and she thinks he's a jerk. But he's still this globe-trotting journalist who brings truth and justice to the world. And I'm just a guy."

"A guy with a dog. Don't discount Rochester's power."

"That's comforting," I said, as he turned onto River Road. "Have you heard anything about this ship thing, through police channels?"

"The Stewart's Crossing PD generally steers clear of international incidents," he said. "You want to talk about the rash of burglaries in Crossing Estates, that, I've heard about. Cruise ships? Nothing."

"Van has this cockamamie idea that there's spy equipment on the ship."

"Cockamamie? That one of those college professor words?" He laughed.

"I'm not a professor anymore. At least not now. And cockamamie is a word my father used to use."

He nodded. "Mine, too. Along with a bunch of others too colorful to repeat. Seriously, she's in Albania?"

"As far as I know. I haven't heard from her since she was boarding the plane in Rome."

There were no other dogs at the park, which was a surprise for a Sunday afternoon. We opened the gate and then let Rochester and Rascal off leash to run around. Rick and I sat on a wrought-iron bench at one end of the park.

"So, Lili's gone," he said. "Bummer. I like her."

"She's coming back," I protested. "As soon as this assignment is over. She's the chair of her department, and she'll have classes in the fall."

Rick leaned back. "And she's gone off with her ex."

"She says they only had a brief fling once years ago."

"Aren't you worried they'll have another?"

I realized that I wasn't worried about Van and Lili fooling around. What really scared me was the idea that she'd come back from Albania—but not to me.

I looked up at the sky. A puffy cumulous cloud drifted above us. "Before she left, she told me I had to clean up the house. That while she was gone I should make room for her."

"Meaning you have to get over your past," Rick said. "I had to do that eventually, after Tiffany moved out. I mean, I threw a lot of her shit away right off, but some stuff I kept. I don't know why. Then one day, a couple of years after the divorce was final, I looked up and said, 'I don't need this crap around.' And I got rid of it."

"None of the stuff in my house ever belonged to Mary. It's all the boxes my father left behind."

"Your parents are part of your past," Rick said. "And so's that guy you were back in Silicon Valley, before you got caught clicking your mouse around to places it wasn't supposed to be."

Rick was right. My ill-fated attempt to take care of Mary by hacking her credit records, and then the year I spent as a guest of the California penal system, had changed me in large and small ways. I'd been dealing with those changes, in learning to love Rochester, and then Lili, and coming to understand my compulsion to snoop around online. But maybe there was more work to be done.

I thought about the number of times my father had been creeping into my thoughts. We had always sparred with each other; I was too much of a wise ass, and my father believed it was his job to knock that sarcasm out of me before the world did it. He was an engineer, with a logical mind, and he couldn't understand the intuitive leaps my brain made sometimes. He never understood how I made a living, working with information rather than mechanical drawings and scale models.

I loved him, of course, and I know that he loved me. I was sorry that I'd missed spending more time with him after my mom died, when I was in California and he was back in Pennsylvania. And I had never acknowledged before that I felt terrible about missing his funeral while I was incarcerated.

Rick and I sat on that park bench for a while, both of us lost in thought, until the dogs came romping back demanding to be played with.

After dinner I cleaned up as best I could—I hung a few pieces of my dad's clothing in my closet, and put the rest into a suitcase to take to the thrift shop. The knickknacks found places in my china cabinet or on my bookshelves. I packed a couple of small boxes of stuff I wanted to save but didn't know what to do with. I had one box of my dad's left to unpack, but when I realized it was all paperwork I put it aside.

During the week, I dropped the suitcase at the thrift shop in the center of Stewart's Crossing, and all the trash and recycling was taken away. The house seemed emptier, and I wasn't sure if it was all the stuff, or the fact that Lili was a world away.

I heard from her sporadically—pictures and quick notes—and I followed Van's stories and her photos in the online edition of the *Journal*. Almost all the passengers on the ship had been flown to Athens within a day or two of their arrival in Tirana, but a half-dozen had been detained. Van chased down diplomats and interviewed the members of the crew who were not behind bars. Lili took photos of the ship, the United States embassy, and various diplomats coming and going.

By Friday morning, the story was over. All foreign nationals held in Albania had been repatriated, and the Siren had been made seaworthy. A skeleton crew was to sail it on to Athens for further repairs. No matter how Van tried, he couldn't make the story into more than it was.

While I was eating breakfast an email from Lili came in with her arrival time in Philadelphia the next evening. I wrote right back to say I'd pick her up at the airport. "Lili's coming home, boy," I said, ruffling Rochester's ears. "That's good news!"

But it meant that I'd have to tackle that last box of my father's. When I got home that evening, I took Rochester for a long walk around River Bend. Fixed a complicated dinner, ate, then fed the dog and cleaned up the kitchen. Then I checked my email in case Lili had sent a more recent message.

Finally, there was nothing more to do but open that last box. My dad had kept meticulous records, but his estate was long since settled, so I could throw away his tax returns, his credit card statements and electric bills, all his Medicare statements and medical records.

Toward the bottom of the box I found a sealed envelope with *Noodnik* on it. That was my father's favorite nickname for me. It wasn't until I was a teenager, studying Yiddish at the Jewish Community Center, that I realized it meant 'pest.' But Dad had always said it with affection.

I opened it and found a single sheet of lined paper in my father's handwriting.

Dear Noodnik,

I wish I had told you this story a long time ago. I always thought that you took after your mother, rather than me. You liked to read, like she did, and you never learned to enjoy the pleasure of working with your hands. But now I realize you are more like me than I ever thought. The computer is your tool, and you do things with it that I could never imagine.

But the use of tools requires responsibility. This is something I did not teach you, because the way I learned this lesson was so painful for me. You know you are named for my brother Seth, who died when he was young. But I never told you how he died, because I killed him.

My heart skipped a beat. My father had killed his brother? I had never heard that story, even a faint rumor of it.

You know that when I was a boy, we lived on a farm in Connecticut. My father had a big electric saw he used to cut wood for our fire. From the time I was old enough to, I helped him. By the time I was twelve, I cut all the firewood myself.

My brother Seth was a little noodnik, like you. He was six years younger, always following me around and getting underfoot. One day when I was cutting wood, a chip flew off a log, and landed right in Seth's eye. The force of the saw sent it deep into his head, and before I could even shut off the saw, he was dead.

My parents never blamed me. It was an accident, they said, even though they cried for my brother's loss. Soon after that we left the farm and moved into the city, and we didn't speak much of Seth. But I resolved that I would always treat my tools carefully, and make sure that I never hurt anyone else with them again.

I don't understand what it is you did that sent you to prison, Steven. But I blame myself, because I didn't teach you this lesson. I hope you will forgive me, and know that I will always love you.

It was signed *Love, Dad* in his careful script.

I rocked back on my heels. What a terrible story to have kept inside him all those years. It explained the way he had always been so careful with his tools, and the way he had kept me away from them when I displayed I had no talent for their use.

All those years, he had been protecting me, not shutting me out.

He had to have written the letter after I went to prison. I wondered when he had intended me to read it. At his funeral?

Soon after, when I packed up the house? It was just an accident of fate that the letter had been packed away with all that other paperwork, and I'd only stumbled on it now.

But I had always believed that the universe did things for us and to us at its own pace. Why had this letter come to me now, when I was trying to put the past behind me and make a new future with Lili? Was this to be my final understanding of my father, my last reconciliation with him?

I doubted that. I knew I would hear his voice in my head until my own death, all those things he had told me about the world and how it worked, those colloquial Yiddish expressions, and the memory of those everyday things he did that demonstrated his love.

Despite all he had done for me, my father wasn't open enough with me—he had kept this secret to himself, though it must have caused him great pain. The lesson in it, if there was one for me, was that I had to open myself up to Lili more. Not just by getting rid of these boxes, or by making peace with my past. But by resolving not to keep secrets, to reveal the darkest parts of my heart and receive some absolution in the process.

I sat there, my arms crossed over my chest, until Rochester came over to me. But he didn't want me to pet him; he kept nosing against the sofa and whimpering.

"What's the matter, boy?" I asked, getting down on my hands and knees. "You have a toy under there?"

His favorite blue plastic ball was there, and I reached in for it. That's when I saw Lili's missing brown-and-yellow butterfly barrette, too.

"Look what you found, boy," I said, holding it in my hand as I stood up. I looked around my living room. It felt open and welcoming, ready for Lili to return.

Story 2: Dog Forbid

Part 1 – Holiday Plans

Squirming and struggling to escape my grip, my eighty-pound golden retriever indicated he'd had enough of beauty treatments. "Hold on, Rochester," I said. "I'm not finished brushing you."

His toenails scratched against the tile floor of my kitchen, and his long plumy tail whapped against the refrigerator with a staccato beat. But I was determined to hold onto him, using the refrain of *Star Trek* geeks everywhere. "Resistance is futile, puppy. You will be groomed."

From the living room, I heard my girlfriend Lili snort. "That dog has you wrapped around his little paw, and he knows it," she called.

"And there's something wrong with that?" I asked.

She didn't answer, just snorted again.

It took a lot of work to keep Rochester healthy and handsome. I used a special comb to pull loose hair from his undercoat, and after a session I often had enough fine strands to spin into wool and make a sweater. I brushed his teeth, trimmed his nails, and cleaned out his ears. Goldens are high-maintenance dogs, but they more than make up for the work with their beauty, brains and loving disposition.

I finished combing the curly hairs behind his ears and let him up, and he scrambled away, leaving a trail of fine golden hairs in his wake. I got the vacuum cleaner out and picked up the hair, and as I was wrapping the cord back around the machine Lili asked, "Have you seen this article in the *Wall Street Journal* online? Van is in Lancaster doing an expose on Amish puppy mills."

I looked over at Lili. She was three years older than I was, in her mid-forties, with a heart-shaped face, a very kissable mouth, and red-framed glasses. She was a couple of inches shorter than my six-foot-one and we both had brown hair, though hers shaded more toward auburn and mine was flecked with gray.

We discovered, soon after we met, that we'd both lived in New York at the same time, in the early 1990s, when she was working as a photographer and I was in graduate school at Columbia, but we hadn't met until she'd come to Eastern College to chair the fine arts department.

We'd been living together for almost a year by then, and I was still marveling at how lucky I was to have her in my life.

"Van Dryver?" I asked. "Your ex-boyfriend?"

"Steve."

"I know, I know," I said. "He was never your boyfriend. Just a fling. But you keep in touch with him." I put the vacuum back in the hall closet and joined Lili on the sofa.

"I read his articles," Lili said. "He's a good writer. And I think you'd be interested in this piece. I'll email you the link."

I opened my iPad and got the message from Lili, and then read the article, the first of a series about dog breeding operations in the Amish country of Pennsylvania. The opening paragraph was a real heart-breaker.

Hidden behind manicured fields and hand-built barns decorated with folk art is a heart-breaking story of animal cruelty. Sad puppies live behind bars in row after row of cages. They never have the chance to run or play, to feel solid ground beneath their feet or sprawl happily in front of a fireplace. They never experience an owner's love.

"This is so sad," I said to Lili.

"And horrifying."

I read on.

At one notorious breeding operation, dozens of cages are attached to the sides of barns, raised a few feet about the ground. They have wire floors so the urine and excrement fall to the concrete below and can be hosed away. Some of the dogs howl in agony, while others cower against the back of their cages in fear. The smell is appalling.

I shook my head. "I can't believe we're supposed to go out to Pennsylvania Dutch country tomorrow. Maybe we should cancel."

A few weeks before, I'd stopped by my friend Mark Figueroa's antique store in the center of Stewart's Crossing, looking for Hanukkah presents for Lili.

"I'm glad you came by," he said, as I browsed his eclectic collection of Bakelite jewelry, Fiesta ware, and porcelain knickknacks. "I've been thinking about Christmas. Do you guys have plans?"

I shook my head. "Christmas has never been a big holiday for either of us. We'll probably just order Chinese food, in the traditional celebration of our people. You going to Joey's parents' house?"

Mark's boyfriend Joey Capodilupo worked with me at the Friar Lake conference center, where I ran programs and he managed the property. He came from a big Italian-American family with deep roots in the area.

"Joey's aunt is having everyone for a big dinner but she's allergic to dogs, so he can't bring Brody and doesn't want to leave him alone all day."

Joey had a year-old golden retriever puppy who was Rochester's bosom buddy.

"And honestly, I'm not thrilled to fend off all his aunts and uncles and cousins asking us if we're going to get married, now that it's legal."

Mark lived in an apartment upstairs from his antique shop, but from what I understood he'd been staying most nights with Joey as their relationship solidified.

He leaned forward and rested his arms on his counter. He was freakishly tall, nearly six-foot-six, and skinny as a bamboo shoot. "Joey's had this thing about Amish Christmas since he was a kid, so we thought we might sneak out to Pennsylvania Dutch country for the holiday. You think you and Lili would want to come with us?"

"What about the dogs?" I knew Joey would never agree to leave Brody in a kennel. I felt the same way about Rochester.

"I found a dog-friendly motel," Mark said. "And a restaurant that serves Christmas dinner on an outdoor patio with a glass roof and warmers. We could take the dogs out to dinner with us."

I had checked with Lili, and she thought it would be fun. We'd arranged our schedules to leave the next afternoon, Wednesday, so we could do some sightseeing on the way. But because of that puppy farm article I wasn't sure I wanted to go.

"We can't cancel at the last minute," Lili said. "And besides, you can't let one bad apple tarnish a whole community. You of all people should know that."

Lili was right. During my time as a guest of California's penal system, I'd gotten to know a lot of people I might never have met otherwise. I had become well aware of the way people judged others, both in and out of prison.

I'd worked hard to turn my life around, and Rochester and Lili had been a big part of that. Lili was right that I had to grant the same pass to others. Most of the people in Amish country probably found puppy mills as awful as I did.

I went back to Van's article.

The Amish don't have the sentimentality that most people associate with dogs; they treat these canines like livestock. Their argument is that if it's all right to raise cows, pigs and sheep for human use, why treat dogs any differently?

The dogs they own are valuable commodities. The females are forced to have litter after litter until they can no longer breed. A few males are kept around for the express purpose of mating. When the dogs can no longer function as needed, they are sold as pets or disposed of.

I shivered. The protestation of humane treatment reminded me of the evil ways humans had treated others in history, from slavery to gas chambers, as if those other tribes or races were less valuable than those in power.

According to Van, it was a lucrative business, selling the puppies en masse to unsuspecting pet stores. After a while, I couldn't read any more. "Don't send this link to Mark and Joey," I said to Lili. "Joey will freak out."

As I turned the pad off and put it on the bookshelf, Rochester came over to nuzzle me. Maybe he knew I was upset, or maybe my putting away an electronic device was a signal that I was available to deliver some puppy love. Either way worked for me.

I got down on the floor beside him, and he rested his head in my lap while I scratched him behind the ears, then rubbed his belly. After a while it was time for his walk, and we strolled beneath a canopy of leafless trees, Rochester sniffing the brown grass and the occasional evergreen.

He tugged me forward, up onto one of my neighbor's lawns, and started to hunch over. I hadn't expected him to need to poop, so I hadn't brought a bag with me. But he quickly changed his mind and pulled onward.

"Very funny, puppy," I said. "You think you're so clever, putting one over on me."

He looked up at me with a doggy grin, then pulled ahead.

Neil S. Plakcy

Part 2 – Dog-Friendly

The day before Christmas, Lili and I packed the car for the trip to Lancaster. We had to drive down US 1, the road my father had called "Useless One," to get to the Turnpike entrance, and it was jammed with every kind of big box store, car dealer and fast food chain. If you couldn't buy it along that stretch of road, then you probably didn't need it.

Of course the roads were always under construction—I could even remember my father cursing about it as we drove to one of his favorite seafood restaurants, a hole in the wall called Under the Pier that surprisingly still existed.

"Oh, I almost forgot to tell you," Lili said, with a kind of studied falseness in her voice that I twigged to right away. "I hope you don't mind but I emailed Van after I read his story yesterday. He's in Lancaster, and he has no plans for Christmas, so I invited him to join us."

Lili had assured me many times that she had no interest in Van Dryver besides maintaining a professional friendship, so I knew I had nothing to be jealous of. But he was still a good-looking, globe-trotting investigative reporter, and I had to tamp down my own insecurity when it came to him. Though I thought he was a pompous twit, I had to be nice to him for Lili's sake.

So I said, "Sure, no problem. The holidays are all about sharing."

I had a feeling Lili knew I was being just as false as she'd been. But that's life with someone else. You smile and smooth things over and move on, right?

It was a relief to leave behind the snarls of traffic and endless red lights for the faded greens and browns of the highway verges. Traffic flowed smoothly past bland sound-buffering walls that protected the neighboring areas from too much highway noise. We were isolated from any connection to the surrounding area, as if we'd driven into some kind of bubble that would eventually deliver us to our destination.

We got off the turnpike at the exit for Route 222, then followed a series of signs showing the silhouette of a horse and buggy and the words "Share the Road." We ended up behind a square black Amish buggy with a red-and-orange hazard triangle on the back and a bumper sticker that read "I'd rather be plowing."

The buggy was being pulled by a proud-stepping roan horse with a black mane, and when they finally turned off onto a side road I saw the driver was a young-looking Amish guy with a long beard, and there were a half-dozen boys with round-brimmed straw hats packed in with him.

The dog-friendly inn Mark had found was called the Distelfink, named after a kind of stylized bird popular in Pennsylvania Dutch folk art. It was a low-slung roadside motel with a picture of a schnauzer on the sign, with the words "pet-friendly."

I saw Joey's truck in the parking lot. "The boys are already here," I said. "Keep an eye on Rochester in case he wants to go find his friend before we check in."

"Better yet, I'll check us in and you can manage the dog."

I leaned over and kissed her cheek. "Works for me."

My golden just woofed from the back seat. As soon as I let him out, holding tight to his leash, he sniffed around a stand of maples at the edge of the parking lot and I imagined he was looking for Brody's scent.

Rochester had a nose for detection; in several cases he had led me to clues that I had been able to pass on to my friend Rick, a homicide detective in our hometown of Stewart's Crossing, nestled against the banks of the Delaware River, about forty-five minutes northeast of Philadelphia. I enjoyed the snooping; I was trying to channel my curiosity away from hacking and into more legal endeavors.

Rochester lifted his leg and peed copiously then romped around me, trying to wind his leash around my legs. Lili came back out of the office with our keys, and we walked down to our first-floor room. It was generic, but it had a king-sized bed for Lili and me and a big cushion on the floor for Rochester. Add in a working bathroom and a television with HBO and cable, and that was about all we needed.

Joey knocked on our door as we were getting settled. He was a good-looking guy in his early thirties, a couple of inches over six feet with broad shoulders. I thought he and Mark made a good pair, partly because they were both so tall.

"Our room is a couple of doors down. Can we bring Brody in to say hello?"

"Of course," I said, and Joey leaned out the door and whistled.

The dogs reunited and we all said our hellos. Brody and Rochester both had the square head and sleek body characteristic of the breed, but Brody's fur was white with a few streaks of gold. At seventy pounds, he was a real handful. He had just celebrated his first birthday and reached sexual maturity, which meant that he'd begun lifting his leg to pee and straining toward every female dog he saw.

He was a couple of inches shorter than Rochester and about ten pounds lighter. Apparently the cream line had a smaller stature, which helped them avoid congenital problems like hip dysplasia.

I loved watching the two of them play. Brody liked to grab Rochester's collar and tow him along. They'd take turns trying to mount each other, or Brody would sprawl on his back with Rochester above him, a symphony in gold and white.

The two dogs were racing around the room. "I hope they can behave while we're out in public," I said.

"I told Brody he'd better be good, or I'd send him to one of those Amish puppy mills," Joey said.

"You know about them?"

"Sure. When I was researching breeders I read all these horror stories. Made me that much more determined to get a dog raised by someone responsible."

I hoped Rochester had had a good upbringing. He'd been a rescue dog when he came to live with my next-door neighbor, Caroline Kelly, and after her death he had moved in with me. Since then we'd become bonded at the hip – almost literally, because the dog followed me everywhere, even when I just got up from my chair for a minute. I called him my Velcro dog. But that's a golden's nature, and Brody was the same way with Joey.

In fact, as soon as Brody got tired he rushed back to his daddy's feet and collapsed there. A minute later, though, he was up and running around again.

Lili told the boys she'd invited another guest to join us for dinner the next day, and though Mark raised an eyebrow toward me, they both said that was fine with them.

"What are we going to do for dinner tonight, though?" Joey asked. "I don't think it's a good idea to leave both the dogs here until they've had a chance to get accustomed to being away from home."

"Why don't we get take-out?" Mark asked. "Steve told me that Jews like to eat Chinese at Christmas, and we passed a place nearby that delivers."

He found the website for House of Ho, and we all looked at the menu together online. Their specials appeared to a melding of Amish and Chinese cuisine – and not in a good way.

"Egg foo young with minced Lebanon Bologna?" I read. "Ho No. That sounds awful."

"What about Scrapple Chow Mein?" Mark asked. "What is that?"

"Scrapple is a mush of pork trimmings with cornmeal and flour, molded into a gelatinous mass, then sliced and pan-fried," I said. "My dad called it a heart attack on a plate. I wouldn't eat it as a kid and I'm not about to start as an adult."

"Hold on," Lili said. "They have ordinary Chinese food, too."

We'd brought food for the dogs, and we fed them, and Mark and I took them for a walk while we waited for the delivery

"I'm really glad you guys could come with us," Mark said. "This is Joey's and my first trip together and it's easier having friends around."

"Come to think of it, this is my first vacation with Lili, too." I looked at Mark. "How are things going with you guys?"

"It's a little rough sometimes," Mark admitted. "I've lived on my own for years and I'm kind of set in my ways. And you know Joey with Brody – that dog can do no wrong." He smiled. "But I really do love the guy, and Brody too. So we make things work."

"It's the same with Lili and me," I said. "This is her third time around the block, and my second, and we both have a lot of baggage."

"She was married twice before?" Mark asked.

"Yeah, and she had other boyfriends along the way," I said. "One of whom will be joining us for dinner tomorrow."

"That reporter guy? Won't that be weird for you?"

I shrugged. "It is what it is. Don't you and Joey have exes who show up now and then?"

"Not on your life," Mark said. "They're exes for a reason. If one of Joey's showed up I'd probably claw his eyes out." He laughed. "Or at least urge Brody to pee on him."

"Let's hope we don't come to that tomorrow with Van," I said.

We ate at a big round table in Mark and Joey's room. After dinner, Lili and I went back to our room with Rochester. Since we expected most places would be closed on Christmas Day, we thought we'd relax in the morning, and to that end we'd brought a lot of reading material with us. Lili had a couple of months of photography magazines to catch up on, and I had several mystery novels loaded on my Kindle.

We read for a while, then I took Rochester for his before-bed walk. It was a completely different atmosphere from River Bend, our gated community. Traffic whizzed by on the main road beside us, semi-trailers applying their hydraulic brakes and motorcycles revving their engines. We stayed on the grassy verge, navigating past fast-food wrappers and shreds of newspaper as Rochester looked for something natural to pee on.

On the way back home he grabbed a piece of paper in his mouth, and I didn't see it until we'd gotten back into the parking lot, under the halogen streetlight. I tugged it from his mouth, where he'd already chewed half of it away. It looked like a flyer for a farm that sold puppies. "Not happening, buddy," I said. "You can play with Brody but you're not getting a puppy of your own."

I crumpled the flyer and tossed in the trash, and we went inside. We had brought food with us for breakfast, and the room had a coffee maker that could boil water for tea and hot chocolate, so we were set. The boys ended up at a McDonald's getting drive-through.

Part 3 – Van Makes an Entrance

The dogs played together for a while in the morning. Then at two o'clock we left for the restaurant. There wasn't enough room in my car or Joey's truck for all of us and the dogs, so we caravanned. We took a country road out of Lancaster, past brown fields that had been laid down for winter and a red-planked covered bridge over a narrow creek, with stone abutments and a peaked black roof. It was only a single lane wide, and as we passed a horse and buggy came out of it, this one carrying only a very young-looking husband and wife. I wondered if they were on their way to a big family Christmas.

My parents both had siblings, and were close with their own first cousins as well, so I grew up surrounded by family. My great-aunts and great-uncles lived just across the Delaware River from us in Trenton, and every Saturday my mother would stop by to visit at least one of them while she ran her errands. I remember sitting in my great-aunt's kitchen, puzzling over the Yiddish language newspaper, *The Forward*, which was written in Hebrew characters.

That great-aunt hosted a family Seder every year. One of my aunts had claimed Thanksgiving, and another Christmas. We traveled all over New Jersey for birthday parties, bar mitzvahs, weddings and funerals. Though I was an only child, I never felt alone.

How had I ended up with no family around me, when my childhood had been so full? My grandparents, great-aunts and great-uncles had all died by the time I was a teenager, and now most of my aunts and uncles were gone, too, or moved to retirement communities in Florida. My cousins had spread around the globe, from an NGO worker in Namibia to a translator in Paris to a computer geek in Seattle, with others interspersed all over the country.

Almost all of them had children of their own. I followed some of them on Facebook, where they bragged about the accomplishments of their kids, documented their vacations, and posed together at family reunions. I had lost touch with most of them as Mary and I tried and failed to have a family, and then faded off the radar when I went to prison.

I had a couple of cousins left in New Jersey, and perhaps it was time to begin mending relations and joining them for happy occasions. I'd see.

The sky was gray and overcast, and the leafless trees along the roadside contributed to a grim atmosphere. In the distance I saw a couple of black crows circling over a lone pine tree, and dozens of small birds like wrens or finches roosted on the power lines above us.

Fortunately, when we pulled up at the restaurant it was lit with tiny fairy lights over the doors and around the windows, and the glow from inside was welcoming. A bluebird darted past us, toward a bird feeder by the side of the building, where a flock of fat mourning doves pecked the ground. A big banner hung over the front door, wishing us a blessed Christmas.

I took Lili's hand in mine and squeezed. She and Rochester were the chief blessings in my life, and I was grateful for both of them.

A hostess greeted us at the door, wearing a knee-length dark blue dress, her blonde hair piled beneath a starched white cap. "Welcome to dinner," she said. She leaned down to pet both dogs. "Welcome to you, too."

She led us past the entrance to the main dining room to the outdoor patio at the rear of the building. It was pleasantly warm, thanks to a glass covering and tall warming stands near each table. Most of the dozen tables were occupied, several parties accompanied by dogs, and Brody strained to go visiting, but Joey kept him on a tight leash.

A small plate of rawhide dog chews sat in the center of our table, and once we'd been seated we kept the dogs occupied with them. "I thought you were having a friend join us," Joey said to Lili.

"Van likes to make an entrance," she said. "He'll be here soon, I'm sure."

We ordered a bottle of white wine and began nibbling on a platter of crudités. A few minutes later, a man in a Burberry trench coat, with a scarf in the matching plaid, and a deerstalker hat like Sherlock Holmes, stepped into the doorway and looked around the room.

He posed there for a moment as if deciding to grace us with his presence. Lili waved at him and he nodded, then walked over to us. I could see people in the room looking at him like he was someone special. The two women at the table next to us were trying to figure out where they recognized him from – as if he was a movie star or something.

He made a big production of shedding all his layers and settling in with us. "Very quaint," he said, as Lili scooted her chair aside so Van could sit next to her.

After introductions had been made, Joey asked him about his article. "I understand you're researching puppy mills. Do you think they can be stopped?"

"I can't talk about an article while I'm working on it," Van said, in what I thought was a pompous tone. "I need to save my words for the story."

I wanted to ask how he could interview people if he couldn't talk about what he was writing, but I restrained myself. He was Lili's friend, and I had to be polite.

He didn't mind talking about his past stories, though. "You'll be interested in this, though," he said to Joey and Mark. "I was in California reporting on the legalization of same-sex marriage and I met some fascinating people."

As we nibbled fresh rolls and hand-churned butter, he told us about the colorful characters he'd interviewed. I had to admit he was a good storyteller, even though the point of every story seemed to be what an excellent investigative journalist he was.

He told more stories as we dug into the farm-grown turkey, chestnut stuffing, and spinach raised right there on the farm and creamed together with butter from local cows. Van segued into a story about the farm-to-table movement in restaurants, and by the time the homemade pumpkin pie with fresh whipped cream arrived, I was annoyed that no one else had much chance to talk. After all, we'd come on this vacation with Joey and Mark, our friends, and I wanted to hear from them now and then.

The dogs ate specially prepared platters of ground turkey mixed with sweet potatoes, cranberry sauce and gravy. These Amish were very kind, and their attention to our canine companions made me question the idea that other in the community treated their dogs like livestock. I wondered if Van had exaggerated anything in his story. He carefully choose his words to create a particular picture, even in the simplest story to us.

Rochester and Brody were on their best behavior, and by the time they'd been fed they were happy to collapse beside us and sleep. I felt the same way by the time dinner was over.

In the parking lot after the meal, Lili asked, "Would you mind if I went over to Van's hotel to have a nightcap with him? We have a lot to catch up on, and that's about the only place that's going to be serving tonight."

"No problem," I said. "Rochester and I can squeeze in with Brody and the boys. Just drive carefully." I kissed her cheek, and she walked off with Van.

"You're a nice guy, Steve," Joey said, as we walked to our truck. "You really don't mind Lili going off with her ex like that?"

"I know Lili, and I know Van, though of course not as well. Sure, I wouldn't put it past him to make a move on Lili. But she's more like to slap him than kiss him. Wouldn't you trust Mark with one of his exes?"

"Are you kidding?" Joey said. "There's only one reason a gay man spends time alone with an ex. And I'd cut Mark's dick off if I found out he was using it with someone else."

"Back at you, sweetheart," Mark said, and he smiled and gripped Joey's hand.

Maybe it was that Lili and I were ten or more years older than Joey and Mark, or that we'd been together longer than they had, but I was glad we trusted each other and could avoid some drama.

Then I squeezed into the rear of Joey's truck and my big dog jumped up on me. I realized that the real source of drama in my life was right there with me. "Yes, Rochester," I said. "I'm right here, and I love you." I snuggled my nose into the soft fur along his neck. "But you're still not getting a puppy of your own."

Part 4 – Slipped Away

Lili was back at the motel about an hour later. "I thought Van told some interesting stories at dinner," I said, as she prepared to join me in bed.

"All of them about himself in the end," she said. "But once I got him away from an audience we had a good conversation. He wants to get a dog, which is good emotional progress for him. He'll have to care about something other than himself."

"Doesn't he travel too much to take care of a dog?"

"He thinks there might be a book in this puppy mill situation. He's tired of traveling and wants to settle down somewhere and work on one project for a long time. He's going to be fifty soon, and being an investigative reporter is a hard life."

She slid into bed beside me. "I'm glad about the choices I made. I wish him the best."

"And am I one of those choices you made?" I turned to her and smiled.

"One of the best," she said, and kissed me. Then Rochester jumped up on the bed between us.

The next morning Lili and I ate breakfast in our room. We were surprised by a banging on the door. I opened it to Mark, who looked stressed.

"Thank God you guys are here. Have you seen Brody?"

"What do you mean? Wasn't he with you?"

"One of the guys who work here told us about a diner that was open for breakfast, and we there," Mark said. "We left Brody in the room. When we got back, the door had been jimmied open and both of our iPads were gone, along with Brody."

For a moment I thought he was implying that the dog had absconded with the electronics. He was a smart puppy, but not that smart. "Have you called the police?"

"Yeah, there's an officer on the way. But we have to look for Brody in case he slipped out of the room while the burglars were inside."

"They advertise this as a dog-friendly motel, right? Maybe Brody got too friendly with someone else's dog. Right, Rochester? Hope the female doesn't sue for puppy support."

"I can only hope that's so," Mark said. "But Joey is beside himself."

I knew how Joey felt; if anything had happened to Rochester, I'd have been the same way. Dog forbid that should ever come to pass.

The three of us went down to Mark and Joey's room. Joey was sitting on the bed. He was such a happy-go-lucky guy that it was odd to see him so distressed. "I know he's not lost," he insisted. "Somebody must have stolen him." Rochester went up to Joey and nuzzled his hand. Joey looked down at him and began to cry.

Mark sat beside Joey and put his arm around Joey's shoulder. "We're going to get him back."

I sat on a chair across from them. "What makes you think Brody was stolen?" I asked.

"After we got back, we went outside and I called for Brody. He always comes when I call him," Joey said, sniffling. "That's the first thing I taught him. We walked all around the motel, and then up and down the highway in each direction for at least half a mile. I'm sure he'd have come back by now if he'd just gotten out. Whoever stole our iPads must have stolen him too."

"Let's back up," I said. "What time did you go to breakfast?"

Mark looked at Joey. "Like eight o'clock? When we got back around nine we saw that the door had been jimmied."

"You said one of the employees recommended the restaurant, right?" I asked. "That means he knew you were leaving your room. You should tell the cops to talk to him."

Two uniformed officers, a man and a woman, showed up a few minutes later. Lili, Rochester and I stayed in the background as Joey and Mark explained what had happened.

"Unfortunately, we've seen a lot of thefts from these old motels," the female officer said. Her name tag read Stoltzfus – a solid Amish name. "The door locks are easy to pick, and the thieves use gloves and get in and out fast."

The male officer's name was Hagen. "Usually these guys are after electronics," he said. "Your dog probably slipped away while the door was open. Have you called the Lancaster County SPCA? Someone could have picked him up already and taken him there."

Officer Stoltzfus added, "You should have some posters printed up with your dog's picture, put them up along the road. Maybe he got into somebody's yard. Has he been neutered?"

Joey shook his head. "They'd have to neuter me before I let them neuter Brody."

"There you go," she said. "He could have sniffed a female in heat and taken off."

"You'll talk to the guy who told Joey and Mark where to go for breakfast?" I asked. "If he knew they were going out to eat, he could have broken in or tipped off whoever did."

Joey and Mark described the guy, and the two officers left.

"Is Brody micro-chipped?" I asked. "Because if he shows up at the shelter they'll read the chip and contact you."

"When I took him in to the vet's after I got him she was out of chips so she said to bring him back. I just haven't gotten around to it. I was going to do it when I take him in for his one-year checkup next week." He started to cry again. "This is all my fault. I should have had him chipped right away. And I never should have brought him out here."

"It's not your fault," I said. "Shit happens in the world. All we can do is clean it up. And a microchip wouldn't matter if he was stolen, only if he ended up at a shelter."

Joey shivered. Mark tried to hug him but Joey pushed him away.

Part 5 – Action Plans

"Do you have a picture of Brody?" Lili asked Joey.

"He has a hundred of them on his phone," Mark said.

"I'll get my laptop, and Joey and I can put together a poster," Lili said.

I turned to Mark. "I saw a lot of antique stores on my way here. You could call any of them that are open and tell them Brody's missing, and ask them to be on the lookout. Ask if they know anybody who might deal in stolen dogs. Any rumors they've heard, people they know who got a cheap deal on a dog?"

"And you said Brody hasn't been neutered, so maybe somebody took him to use in breeding," Lili said. "He's a purebred golden retriever, right? He'd be worth a lot of money as a stud. Somebody could create fake papers for him and sell the puppies."

"We should check for golden breeders in the area," I said. "I can go online and do that. Maybe there's even a golden rescue group in the area. We can notify them and see if they have any information on sketchy breeders. Since there's no Wi-Fi here, I'll go to that coffee shop down the road."

Mark started making calls, and Lili and Joey got to work on a poster. I left Rochester there to keep Joey company and drove down the street to the coffee shop, ordered a drink for myself and set up my laptop.

A purebred golden like Brody, even without his papers, could bring top dollar for resale or breeding. Brody had been a pricy puppy—over two grand plus shipping. Someone who didn't want to pay that much might be able to overlook the dog's provenance.

As soon as I had online access I found a couple of local websites that advertised golden retriever puppies and wrote down their phone numbers. Then I looked for information on how to find lost dogs. There was nothing there I hadn't figured out already, and the news wasn't encouraging; with every minute that passed the chances of Brody getting hit by a car or suffering some other mishap grew greater and greater.

Though I hated the idea, I called Lili. "Can you speak to Van and see if he has any leads we can use? Any puppy mills that sell goldens?"

"One step ahead of you," she said. "I made the call and he's on the case."

I went back to Van's article, then kept on looking at other sites. A TV news program had done an exposé on puppy mills, and I watched the whole broadcast, even though it turned my stomach.

I shuddered at the thought that Brody might have been dognapped by one of those operations, or that whoever had broken into Joey and Mark's room to steal their electronics had noticed the dog and scooped him up to be quickly sold.

After a while, I couldn't read any more. Lancaster was the puppy mill capital of the United States, and the sooner we found Brody and get out of there the better.

By the time I got back to the motel, Lili and Joey had returned from the copy center with fifty copies of poster and a staple gun. They were ready to go out and paper the town.

Mark pulled me aside. "Did the people you talked to know anything?" I asked.

"Nothing," he said. "But that guy we thought worked here? Turns out we were mistaken. There's nobody who works here who fits his description, and the police think you may have been right when you said he was watching us."

"But that doesn't mean he or his accomplices stole Brody," I said. "You guys should go out and put those posters up anyway."

"It's a waste of time," Joey said. "The best I can hope for is that Brody will get a good home with someone else."

"Come on, sweetie," Mark said. "It'll give us something to do."

Part 6 – Companion Puppy

"We need to put Rochester on the case," I said. "He knows Brody's scent. Maybe he can help us find him."

I began to think about how we could use Rochester to help us find Brody, and remembered that people who were looking for a companion puppy often took their dog with them to breeders. "You guys go put up those posters. Lili and I are going to take Rochester and look for breeders, pretending we're shopping for a dog."

Rochester sniffed and peed again outside the motel, and then jumped into the back seat. We headed toward Lititz along narrow country roads with more "share the road" signs and more buggies.

I rolled down the back windows so Rochester could stick his head out, his golden fur flying like Tibetan prayer flags from his head. I was happy to get in line behind a buggy, because it let us drive slowly, looking for signs that might lead us to this puppy mill.

Suddenly Rochester started barking. "What's the matter, boy?" I asked.

"He must smell something," Lili said, peering forward. "See, up there on the right? There's a little sign that says *Puppies for Sale*."

"You are such a smart dog," I said, reaching behind me to ruffle Rochester's fur.

Eyes back on the road, I turned into the narrow dirt road and climbed a hill, then dropped down to where a big white clapboard farmhouse nestled in a dell, flanked by a couple of tall oaks. The farmhouse was three stories tall, with dormer windows and a broad front porch, and looked like it could be on a postcard.

We parked behind an open buggy. Several horses grazed in a field beside us, but the smell that rose on the air was more redolent of dog than horse.

I kept a close hold on Rochester's leash as a boy of about ten came out of the front door. He wore a round-brimmed black hat, a white shirt and suspenders holding up dark pants. "Help you?" he asked.

"We're looking for a dog," I said. "Another golden retriever. You have any for sale?"

"I'll get my pa," he said, and he hurried around the corner.

"You think Brody could be here?" Lili whispered.

"If he is, Rochester will find him," I said.

The boy returned a couple of minutes later with a man of about my age, with the same black hat as his son, but a bushy black beard. "You looking for a dog?" he asked.

I nodded. "Another golden. Hope you don't mind that we brought ours with us. We want to make sure both dogs can get along."

"I have one litter of goldens," he said. "Follow me."

We walked behind him. Rochester was easy on his leash, which made me think that perhaps we were on the wrong trail, and that Brody wasn't there. But we had to follow through on the lead.

"This is state of the art," the man said, as he opened the door. The smell was almost overpowering of dogs and feces, and the noise of all that barking and whimpering was crazy, but he seemed oblivious to it all. Cages lined both walls of the building, about three feet above ground. "My dogs live on plastic sheets, and their waste falls right through to the ground and gets swept away. I make sure they get to exercise on real floors, too. Some of these breeders, the dogs can barely walk when you get 'em home."

We both smiled politely, though I was horrified at the conditions. Three or four puppies shared each cage, all kinds of breeds from Pomeranians to labs to tiny teacup puppies barely bigger than your hand. "Goldens are over here in the whelping bins," the man said.

Eight tiny puppies, looking more like piglets than dogs, clustered around an exhausted looking female. They were all a gorgeous shade of gold, and I could see that they'd garner big money from a pet store. "We were hoping for one of the cream-colored ones," I said. "You have any in that shade? They're supposed to be healthier than the gold."

I leaned down and chucked Rochester under the chin. "No offense to you, puppy."

He shook his head. "My gold puppies are very healthy. Get both parents checked for hip and elbow dysplasia and eye problems. They're the healthiest puppies you'll find."

Rochester was strangely quiet, as if the presence of so many of his kind had overwhelmed him. I told the farmer we'd think about another gold puppy, and he led us outside.

It was such a relief to be back out in the fresh air. Rochester strained at his leash and I figured that being around so many other dogs made him need to pee. My grip on the leash must have slackened, because suddenly Rochester had pulled away from me and was bounding across the grass. "Rochester!" I called. "Come back!"

My beautiful dog was poetry in motion as he galloped away, his legs moving in sync, his fur flying. Four legs move a lot faster than two, and though I raced after him, calling his name, he disappeared into a hedgerow at the end of the field.

Part 7 – A Smart Boy

I stopped short, panting for breath. Rochester had disappeared from sight, and I had no idea where he was going.

Lili caught up to me. "What got into him?"

I shook my head. "No idea. He's never done anything like that before."

Her cell phone rang. "It's Van," she said. "I should take this."

She walked off a few feet as I looked around. Where was my dog? Ahead of me was a cornfield, the brown stalks cut and lying on the ground in haphazard piles. The fields were lined by hedgerows of mature trees, both conifers and deciduous, and they looked impenetrable. Once Rochester got into one of those stands of trees, he could have turned right or left, or gone straight ahead, and I had no way of knowing which way.

Lili came back to me. "Van got a tip that one of the breeders on the road to Lititz just got a new white golden puppy this morning. It's a place called Teacup Farm. He texted me the address and he's going to meet us there."

"I should stay here," I said. "What if Rochester comes back?"

Lili looked around. "This is the road to Lititz, right? Maybe he's on his way to that farm where Brody is. Or maybe we'll see him on the road. We can't just stay here."

I was paralyzed. I didn't know what I should do—keep running through these fields looking for my dog, or head out with Lili to find Brody.

Lili put her arm in mine and tugged gently. "Rochester is a smart boy. He'll either find his way back to the motel, or he'll be with Brody somewhere, or we'll find him some other way."

"What if he gets hit by a car? You know him. He's not afraid of anything."

"Fear is different from intelligence," Lili said.

I took a deep breath. In prison, I had learned to let go of things I couldn't control, and this was one of those. "Let's go, then," I said.

I hated to walk away, but I knew my dog and like me, once he was on the trail of a scent he couldn't be persuaded otherwise. Lili and I hurried back to the car, where I made a K-turn my driver's ed teacher would have been proud of. Then we rocketed down the dirt driveway back toward the street.

"Which way should we turn, do you think?" I asked Lili as we approached the road.

"Van said this farm is on road to Lititz, and Lititz is to the right," she said. I followed her hunch, and we climbed a hill. From the top I saw a line of Amish buggies moving slowly ahead of us, and a stream of oncoming traffic so I couldn't pass them.

My fingers were clenched around the steering wheel. "Take it easy, Steve," Lili said. "Rochester's a smart dog. He'll be all right until we get there."

"But what if we're wrong? If we went in the wrong direction? Or if whoever stole Brody gets hold of Rochester. I couldn't stand to have him end up like those poor dogs we saw."

A piece of paper came flying out of the buggy in front of us, and the driver ground to a halt. A boy in his early teens jumped out and went chasing the paper across a field. We couldn't move forward until the buggy did, and there was no shoulder to go around. Cars full of tourists gawking at the buggies crept past us in the other lane, occasionally someone holding a phone out the window to snap a picture.

I drummed my fingers on the wheel. "Come on," I said. I blew the horn, and the driver stuck his left hand out and waved us around, which wasn't going to do me any good until the traffic eased.

Finally the teenager loped back to the buggy with the paper in his hand, and we began moving again. By then there was a line of cars behind us.

"Do me a favor?" I asked. "Can you use your phone to find out how fast a golden retriever can run?"

"Absolutely." She hit a couple of keys and waited for a page to load. "Wow. I had no idea he could be so fast. Twenty to thirty miles an hour."

"And it's been what? Twenty minutes since he took off? So he could be ten miles away by now."

"He'll be all right, Steve." She squeezed my hand.

My car was too old to have a built-in electronic compass, but it wasn't hard to figure out that the road we were on wasn't following a straight line. We curved around hills and past fields, and within a half mile I was completely turned around. What if we weren't going the way we hoped at all? Suppose we kept driving aimlessly around Amish country as something terrible happened to Rochester?

"Take a deep breath, Steve," Lili said. "We'll find the farm."

I did as she said, and around the next corner we saw a hand-painted sign for Teacup Farm. At the top was a photo of a tiny Yorkie inside an oversized coffee cup. The pink ribbon in her hair matched the pink spangles on the cup. We turned in at the driveway and parked in front of a low-slung building called the Adoption Center, in a row with three other cars. Van Dryver was standing beside one of the cars.

"You go into the building and I'll walk around calling for Rochester," I said.

Lili shook her head. "We'll go inside together, see what the place looks like. If it's like the last farm, they'll take us out to where the dogs are. And that's where Rochester will be, if he's here."

We met Van at his rental car. "I've been talking to the guy who cleans up the dogshit. He's fed up with this place. He's the one who told me about the white puppy."

A Litter of Golden Mysteries

"Thanks, Van," Lili said. She kissed his cheek, and I shook his hand.

"Don't thank me until you find the dog. I'm going to wander around, see if I can find my guy."

We went inside. The place was a showroom for dogs; a dozen compartments built into the walls, with wood chips for flooring. Each case was devoted to a different breed: Chihuahuas, Maltese, Pomeranians, Poodles, Yorkies and Shih-Tzus were the purebreds. There were also Malti-Poos, Morkies, Mal-Shis and Taco Terriers.

I wondered what the breeder was doing with a dog like Brody. He was way too big to be bred with any of these dogs. Was he holding him for resale? Or were we on the wrong track?

The air smelled like lemon air freshener, and the glass windows muted the sound of puppies yipping and barking. Each case held at least two or three puppies who either played together or napped. Around us we could see two other couples, one looking at dogs on their own, another talking with a young Amish woman in a white cap and long blue dress, like the hostess at the restaurant.

Another young woman in a similar outfit approached us. "Welcome to the adoption center. Is there a particular type of dog you're interested in?"

"I'm really partial to the Morkies, but my husband wants a pure bred," Lili said. "Do you raise all the dogs here?"

She nodded. "My father has converted two barns to breeding areas," she said. "I can give you a tour if you'd like."

"That would be great," I said.

This was a much more professional operation than the first farm; we followed a flagstone path behind the Adoption Center to a big red barn with open doors.

"That's a beautiful image," Lili said, pointing to the colorful hex sign on the front of the barn, a pair of dancing stallions. "Does it mean something?"

In elementary school we'd studied those decorative signs as part of a unit on Amish culture, and the one thing I remembered was that most Amish didn't use them.

The girl reinforced that impression. "It's a decoration," she said. "The English expect them when they come out here."

"English?" Lili asked.

"Non-Amish people," she said. "Now here's the barn where the puppies are raised once they've been whelped. The whelping pens are in another barn farther back, but we don't take visitors there."

The interior of the barn was a lot like the shed we'd seen at the first farm, and I tuned out while the girl explained the way the puppies were fed and cleaned. I kept looking around for Rochester or Brody. "I'm feeling a little nauseous," I said to the girl. "I'm going out to get some fresh air. Sweetie, you stay here and learn everything, all right?"

Lili nodded and she and the girl walked farther back into the barn. I stepped outside and scanned the grounds. For once in my life I was looking forward to seeing Van Dryver. I heard some voices in the distance but didn't see anyone. I slipped around the side of the barn and headed toward the whelping building. Had Rochester run all this way? Could he be around somewhere?

An Amish man and a young boy came out of the whelping barn talking. I hid behind a big pine tree until they passed. Rochester must not have been in there, or they'd have seen him.

I couldn't risk calling his name because I didn't want to attract attention to myself. But how could I find him, or Brody? I made a big circuit behind the buildings, alert for any stray Amish who would challenge my presence. I finally found myself approaching a big three-story farmhouse like the one at the farm we'd just visited.

I cautiously walked around the corner of the building. Then I saw Rochester on the ground, curled in front of a window. "Rochester!" I called. "What are you doing here?"

A woman stepped out onto the porch. She was in her forties, wearing the same outfit as the girls at the Adoption Center. "This is private property back here," the woman said. "You need to go back."

"Do you have a white golden retriever puppy here?" I asked. "About a year old, with a gold stripe down his back and gold tips on his ears?"

The woman turned her back on me abruptly and walked inside, the door slamming behind her. Rochester's leash was still trailing behind him, and I grabbed hold of it and waited.

The farmer I'd seen coming out of the whelping barn appeared on the porch. "What do you want here?" he demanded.

"I want my friend's golden retriever puppy," I said. "He's a year old and his name is Brody." I repeated the description I'd given his wife. "He was stolen this morning from the Distelfink Motel in Lancaster."

"Don't have any dog like that here," the man said. "Now you need to git."

Rochester barked and strained toward the porch. "That's not what my dog says," I said. I let him go, and he hurried back over to the window where I'd first seen him. He put his paws up on the sill and barked again. From inside, I heard an answering bark.

"I told you to git. The farmer opened the front door and pulled out a shotgun, which he racked, the noise extra loud in the quiet air.

I ignored him and hurried to where Rochester stood below the window. "Is that Brody?" I called to Rochester, and he woofed and nodded his head.

I turned back to the farmer, who had raised his shotgun to his shoulder and had it aimed at me. "I have reason to believe that you have a stolen dog on your premises," I said.

I'd stood my ground to tougher-looking men in prison and I knew there was no chance the farmer was going to shoot me. I held up my cell phone.

"The police already have a report of Brody's theft. Now, if that dog inside isn't Brody, you just have to show him to me and I'll leave. But if you won't, then I'm calling the cops."

The farmer kept his gun trained on me. He had pushed his flat-brimmed straw hat back on his head so I could see his eyes. They were hard and angry. "I paid three hundred dollars for that dog!"

"Then turn over whoever sold him to you to the cops," I said.

The dog inside the house kept barking. Then Van stepped from around the corner of the house. "And I've got a phone with a video camera and I'm recording this whole encounter," he said. "I'm a reporter for the *Wall Street Journal*, and I know you have a stolen dog inside your house."

"You look like you're running a good operation here," I said to the farmer, lying through my teeth. "It would be a shame to have the cops shut you down. And you know that they will, if they catch you with a stolen dog on your premises."

The door opened behind him and his wife stepped outside, with a white dog on a piece of rope. "Take your dog and git off our property," she said.

She dropped the rope and the dog rushed across to me—or maybe it was to Rochester, who ran back to me.

Even without his collar or tags, I recognized Brody by his distinctive markings, and the way he lunged at me and put his paws up on my waist. "Hello, Brody," I said, ruffling behind his ears. "Your daddy will be glad to get you back."

Brody tried to bite Rochester's ear, and my dog barked sharply at him.

The farmer put his rifle down. "I'm gonna get that Amos Zook," he said. "You can take the dog. You can send the cops if you want but the deputy is my wife's brother-in-law. He'll believe me over a pair of city men even if you do have a fancy telephone."

"All I want is my friend's dog," I said, though I'd registered the name Amos Zook in my brain. Rochester grabbed Brody's rope leash in his mouth and took off, Brody romping along beside him. Van and I hurried after them before the farmer could change his mind. As we rounded the corner of the Adoption Center I saw Lili standing by the car, and we all raced toward her.

I opened the back door and Rochester jumped in. Brody hesitated, but Rochester barked, and I helped the puppy with a boost to his hindquarters. After I got in, I handed Lili my phone, which had Joey's cell number in it.

She called him as I drove back out toward the street, Van following in his rental. "We have your baby," Lili said. "Safe and sound. We're on our way back to the motel."

I heard Joey whoop with joy through the phone's speaker.

"Tell the cop to look for a guy named Amos Zook," I called.

After Lili hung up I asked her to call Van and see if he knew the way back to the motel. He did, and when we came to a lay-by I pulled in and let him take the lead. While we drove I told Lili about how he'd confronted the farmer with his camera, but I didn't mention the farmer was holding a rifle. Aimed at me.

"Van was great," I said. "I take back everything bad I ever said about him."

"I wouldn't go that far. I'm sure this will be great material for Van's article, or his book."

It was late afternoon by the time we got back to the motel. As we pulled up in the parking lot, Joey burst out of the door to his and Mark's room, and Brody went into paroxysms of barking. I got the back door opened just as Joey reached us, and Brody leapt into his daddy's arms.

"How's my Brody boy?" he said into the dog's fur. "Daddy missed you so much." He looked up at us. "I can't thank you guys enough."

"I told you Rochester would come through," Mark said to him.

He told us that he'd called the police and given them Amos Zook's name. "They know who he is, and they've had their eye on him for a while."

Van got out of his car and joined us. "I appreciate what you did," I said, reaching out to shake his hand. "You were pretty awesome."

"To get the best story a reporter has to be fearless," he said, and I forgave him the bluster, though if he kept it up I might have to say something.

"Officer Stoltzfus said she might need us to come by the station tomorrow to see if we can identify him as the man who had told us about that restaurant," Mark said.

"I hope they give him the electric chair," Joey said.

I thought the chances that the guy would serve any time at all were slim, but I didn't say that. Instead I asked, "Did he still have your iPads?"

"Yup. Officer Stoltzfus says we can pick them up tomorrow," Mark said. "And she told me that there's a café a couple of miles away that lets dogs in. I say we all go get some dinner." He turned to Van. "You're welcome to join us, too."

He begged off, something about meeting a source. Mark led the way to the restaurant, where we had a great, celebratory meal, sharing table scraps with both dogs.

The next morning, Mark and Joey identified Amos Zook, and the police said they were well on their way to putting a case together against him. They got their electronics back, and we enjoyed the rest of the weekend, driving around to antique stores, alternating who stayed with the dogs and who got to shop. Lili found a quilt she liked, a white one with an applique pattern of flowers surrounding a square house—with a gold-colored dog lying by the front door.

I thought it was the perfect souvenir for a vacation that had taken a bad turn, but ended well. We caravanned back to

Stewart's Crossing Sunday afternoon. Mark, Joey and Brody took the lead, and I followed, with Lili on the front seat and Rochester sticking his nose between us. It was just the way I liked to ride.

Story 3: Riding the Tiger

I like to read my spam email, because as a somewhat reformed hacker I'm always interested in how bad operators can manipulate online data. I admired the ingenuity of whoever came up with the idea to email all your friends, telling them you've been robbed in a foreign country and need their help to get home. I wondered at the gullibility of anyone who'd consider helping that Nigerian prince get his funds out of his country.

But the bitcoin email I got one Saturday morning in early September, which my ISP didn't flag as spam, was a twist I'd never heard of before.

Bitcoin is a digital currency, created about ten years ago by an anonymous computer genius. You could buy bitcoins using physical currency, or you could earn them by helping to process transactions from other users. Then you could use your capital to buy goods and services online.

A single bitcoin was currently worth somewhere near a thousand dollars. The way one accesses one's hoard of bitcoins is through an address at one of the bitcoin exchanges. It contains a string of alphanumeric characters, but can also be represented as a scannable QR code.

The address is supposed to be unique and secure, but there have been several big cases of theft, and some exchanges have suspended users due to suspected criminal activity. The person emailing me, who identified himself as GrayMarketGary, had had his account suspended and needed the help of another bitcoin user to retrieve the money he had there.

If I would allow him to use my address, he'd reward me with ten percent of what he had in his account – according to him, over a hundred thousand dollars' worth.

It smelled like scam to me. If his account was suspended, there was no way using mine would help him get his money out. Either he didn't know that, or he was trying to get access to my funds, which were pretty minuscule. I'd only dabbled in bitcoin, earning myself a few dozen millibitcoins, or mBTCs, by doing processing work a few years before when I was unemployed and had lots of time on my hands. I hadn't checked lately but my stash was probably worth no more than a few dollars.

From the header for the email, I got the IP address it had been sent from, and then used a geolocation program to figure out where in the physical world the address was located. I was stunned to discover it read 418 Main Street in Stewart's Crossing, PA.

So this scammer was right in my hometown. Interesting. I'd come back to town after the demise of my marriage and a year-long stint in the California prison system for a stupendous hack I'd committed on the three major credit bureaus. Since then I'd tried to keep my nose clean, though occasionally I couldn't resist snooping online, always in the service of a greater good. Or so I justified my actions.

I was curious about another cyber-criminal living close to me. It was a gorgeous day, my live-in girlfriend was out taking photographs, and I had nothing on my agenda, so I decided to take Rochester for a long walk into the center of town. We'd stop at the Chocolate Ear café and sit outside with a café mocha for me and one of Gail's homemade dog biscuits for Rochester. And if we happened to pass by the address on Main Street—well, that would be coincidence, wouldn't it?

Rochester relished any chance to get out into the fresh air, and once we passed the guardhouse at the entrance to River Bend, the community where we lived tucked into an elbow of the Delaware River, he realized we were going for a long walk, and jumped around joyfully, like a demented kangaroo.

"Okay, calm down, puppy," I said, tugging on his leash. "We have a long walk ahead of us and you don't want to get tired out too quickly."

As if that would happen. Rochester had an endless supply of energy, especially when the outdoors was involved. He was about eighty pounds of fur, lolling tongue and wagging tail, his coat a honey gold. The top of his head was as soft as cotton, the straight hair on his back a bit coarser, with occasional whorls I loved to tease with my fingers.

We strolled up to Main Street and turned south, toward the Chocolate Ear. Traffic buzzed along beside us, the ubiquitous SUVs that had replaced the station wagons of my youth, moms ferrying their kids to sports practice or dance class. An older couple on a three-wheeled motorcycle, the woman's long white hair blowing in the wind. Delivery trucks, a van from the Church of the Apostolic Revival, dark-skinned faces peering out the windows like we were caged animals on display.

The buildings along Main Street are a mix of colonial era stone houses and old Victorians, with more modern houses and stores filling the gaps. As we walked, I passed a few landmarks of my childhood. The florist where I used to buy my mother a single carnation, usually because I was apologizing for something. The five-and-dime where I bought penny candy with the leftovers of my allowance was now a doctor's office but I could still remember the display cases filled with wax lips, Turkish taffy, and chocolate cigars and cigarettes in colorful boxes.

While Rochester sniffed and peed, ignorant of my personal history, I scanned for the scammer's address. I was so busy snooping that when he pulled hard on his leash the loop slipped out of my hand, and he was off, chasing a tiger-striped cat down the sidewalk.

"Rochester!" I called, to no avail. When he thinks another animal wants to play, there's no stopping him. My only hope was that the cat would come to a quick halt, raise its back like a Halloween silhouette and hiss, and that Rochester would take the hint.

Instead the cat kept going. I took off after them, but their four legs allowed them both to move a lot faster than my two. The cat jumped up onto the porch of one of the Victorians, then darted through the front door, which was partially open.

Rochester was right behind it.

"Oh, crap!" I hurried up to the Victorian a moment later and bounded up the steps. I knocked on the door. "Hello?"

No answer. From inside I could hear the clicking of Rochester's toenails on the wooden floor. "Rochester!" I called in a low voice. "Come here now!"

He didn't respond. I pushed the door open a little farther and called out again. "Hello? Anyone home?"

The cat meowed, and Rochester woofed. Was that my invitation? There was no way I was going to be able to retrieve my dog without going inside.

I stepped into a gloomy foyer. One of those constant-flowing water bowls for dogs and cats was right inside, though it was empty of water. I heard the rumble of rap music with a deep bass line coming from an open door to my right, and I stepped over to it.

The door led into a room that had been fitted out as an office, with a desk made of a wooden door laid over a pair of short file cabinets. A laptop computer was open on the top, and it appeared that the music was coming from its speakers.

The cat was perched on top of the desk beside the laptop, sitting up on its hind legs. Rochester sat in a similar position on the floor facing it. The cat's empty food bowl rested underneath a pair of windows that looked out at the house next door. On the wall I spotted a couple of framed photos of a dark-haired guy in his late teens or early twenties with the tiger-striped cat on his lap.

"Rochester! You are a very bad dog!" I tried to grab his leash, but he scurried under the desk. The cat meowed and pawed at the laptop.

I moved around to the back of the desk and noticed that the screen saver was dissolving after the cat had touched the keyboard. A series of computations filled the screen—a series that I recognized.

The laptop was running software to analyze a bitcoin block chain – verifying someone else's transaction as a way to earn bitcoins for the laptop's owner.

I hadn't checked the address to the house as I charged in, but it must be where the email sent to me had originated. What were the odds that two people on Main Street in Stewart's Crossing were part of the bitcoin network?

But where was the spammer? Why had he disappeared, leaving his front door open and his computer running? From the faint pong wafting through the room it smelled like the cat's litter box hadn't been changed in a while, and there was no food or water for the poor thing.

Was that why the cat had lured Rochester and me inside? So we could give it the food and water it was missing?

I hesitated. It was quite possible that the spammer was in the house somewhere, and had just been too caught up in his work to take care of the cat.

But something about the loving way the guy looked at the cat in the photos, its elegant pink collar, all the toys on the floor, made me think that wasn't the case.

So I did what I should have done before I even stepped into the house – I called my friend Rick.

Rick Stemper and I had known each other in high school, when we'd been lab partners in chemistry class, but we hadn't become friends until I'd returned to Stewart's Crossing. He was a detective with the Stewart's Crossing Police Department, and Rochester and I had occasionally gotten involved in his cases, because my goofy golden seemed to have a nose for crime.

When Rick answered, I explained the situation. "I don't want to leave without giving the cat some food and water, but there's something spooky about this house and I'm afraid to touch anything."

"For once you're thinking like an intelligent adult. Take the dog back outside and wait for me. I'm at the station now, and I'll be there in about five minutes."

Rochester wasn't willing to leave, splaying his paws, and the cat meowed anxiously, but I managed to drag the dog out to the porch. We sat on the front step, with my hand through Rochester's collar. The cat stayed just inside the front door, watching us closely.

The police station was only a couple of blocks away, at the corner of Main and Hill Streets, so he approached on foot. Rochester barked a couple of welcoming woofs as Rick stepped up onto the porch.

"No one's home?" he asked.

"Nobody answered me," I said. "But I didn't go anywhere other than into the office. I think this is just a first-floor apartment, so there may be somebody upstairs."

"Wait here."

He announced himself at the door, and when he got no answer he walked inside. The cat trailed behind him, and I sat on the step with Rochester by my side, my hand remaining gripped on his collar.

About five minutes later, Rick came back out to the porch. "Nobody home. And it does look kind of suspicious, like the guy ran out in the middle of what he was doing. You know what that stuff is on his computer screen?"

"Bitcoin." I changed my grip from Rochester's collar to his leash, stood up and explained about the spam email I'd gotten, how I'd tracked it to the house.

"You're sure the story you fed me about the cat is true?" he asked. "You didn't just go inside to snoop around because of the email you got?"

Rochester strained to go back into the house. "Swear to God," I said. "What are you going to do?"

Rick sighed. "This is not a police case, Steve."

"Did you look around in there? See all the pictures of the guy and his cat, the certificate on the wall from the cat's breeder? This is not someone who would run off and leave his cat without food and water."

"Yes, I saw that. And I sympathize. But I don't have any authority here."

"What about the cat? Can I at least give it some food and water?"

"You're a private citizen. I can't do anything to stop you. But if I were you, I'd do it and then get out. The guy who lives here is going to come back eventually. And he probably won't appreciate your snooping around."

I disagreed. If anything happened to me, I'd be happy if someone looked after Rochester. "But what if he doesn't? What if something happened to him?"

"Again. Not a police case. At least not until someone who knows him actually reports that he's missing."

He stepped down to the sidewalk. "I've got to get back to the station. Act like the smart guy I know you are, Steve."

He turned his back and began walking away. Yeah, I was a smart guy, and I knew I shouldn't get involved. I wasn't even a cat lover. But I couldn't let someone's prized pet go hungry.

I let go of Rochester's leash and he scampered back into the house. I followed him inside, and found the kitchen. The cat followed me, with Rochester right behind her. A plaque was hung above the sink that read "Shere Khan Rules Here," with a drawing of the tiger I recognized from the animated movie of Kipling's *The Jungle Book*, which I'd seen as a kid.

"Is that your name?" I asked the cat, who wound her way through my legs. "Shere Khan?" She meowed, which I took for a yes.

Her coat was the same orange as the tiger, with dark stripes around her body, and her muzzle and ears were white. She was a beautiful specimen of her breed, whatever it was, and probably quite valuable.

I found a bag of cat food branded by a reality TV chef. Rochester sprawled out in the doorway of the kitchen, and he and Shere Khan watched as I poured dry food into a bowl and then put it down for her. Rochester watched her while she ate and I replaced the water container by the front door. Then I squinched up my nose as I emptied the litter into the trash, sealed the bag up and took it out to the can in the back yard. Then I replaced it with clean stuff.

So Shere Khan was taken care of. But what about her owner? Could I find out where he'd gone by snooping around his laptop?

Of course Rick would frown on that. But this guy wasn't exactly a model citizen, and in my mind the kind of criminal activity he'd been engaging in could have gotten him into trouble.

The kind of trouble I was very familiar with.

After all, who better to help a scammer than a hacker? I went back into the office and sat down at the desk. My fingers tingled with that old familiar anticipation, the yen to go poking into somewhere I didn't belong.

Within a few minutes I knew his real name – Jordan Campo.

A Litter of Golden Mysteries

I knew that he rented the first-floor apartment through a management company, that he had grown up in South Philadelphia, and that he was a student at Bucks County Community College, where he was studying computer science. That he had bought Shere Khan as a kitten from a breeder of Bengal cats.

And that he had been diagnosed with Asperger Syndrome and had a prescription for Risperdal to treat symptoms of irritability.

I knew a little about the syndrome – that people with it had trouble relating to others and responding to social cues, and that they were often obsessed with one or more topics, like dinosaurs or baseball.

Jordan Campo appeared to be obsessed with bitcoin. He had dozens of file folders on his laptop, filled with PDFs and Word documents and Excel spreadsheets, all of them relating to bitcoin. He belonged to a dozen online groups that discussed the topic, and had paid several different entrepreneurs for training. Somewhere along the way he'd picked up the idea that he could scam other bitcoin users, and in one of the spreadsheets I found my name, email, and bitcoin address.

"Son of a bitch," I said out loud, and Rochester looked up from his place on the floor beside me. Shere Khan was across the room on a gold velvet pillow and she didn't react.

I looked at the clock and realized I'd been in Jordan Campo's house for nearly three hours and I was no closer to figuring out what had happened to him. But this had become personal now, because he knew things about me, and I wasn't going to let him get away with that.

I thought there might be a clue in his emails, but he had password-protected the account and I couldn't hack into it without the tools I had on my laptop at home. I wrote down everything about the account on a piece of paper.

I found a couple of loose keys in the desk drawer, and discovered that one of them locked the front door. I left Shere Khan with more food, water, and clean litter and let myself and

Rochester out, locking the door and pocketing the key. I'd come back and check on the cat in a day or two.

Rochester didn't seem willing to leave Shere Khan behind, but I tugged on his leash and once he was outside he was happy to keep on sniffing the bushes and dead branches along Main Street as we walked to the Chocolate Ear.

I hooked his leash around the leg of one of the wrought-iron chairs on the sidewalk in front of the café and went inside. Gail, a cheerful blonde in her late twenties, was behind the counter, and she greeted me warmly. "How's your day going?" she asked, as she began to make my café mocha.

"Kind of weird." I told her about Rochester chasing the cat into the old Victorian. "The poor cat had no food, no water, and a nasty litter box. No wonder she was outside looking for help."

"Nobody was there at all?"

Gail was a Bucks County native, too, so I thought she'd also have seen the pictures my social studies teacher had shown us of Pompeii, the way it looked like time just stopped in the middle of everything.

She nodded and handed me my coffee.

"That's what it reminded me of. Like he just stepped out for a minute but never came back."

"That is spooky. Did you ever find out his name?"

"Jordan Campo," I said. "You know him?"

"There's a guy named Jordan who comes in sometimes. Kind of odd. He never looks you in the eye."

"Sounds like the same guy. I think maybe he has Asperger's. But he's a computer genius."

"Yeah, Mindy says she sees him at the community college sometimes and he's always staring at his phone. One day she saw him walk into a tree because he was so involved."

Mindy was Gail's part-time worker, a teenager who took

college classes and changed her major every semester so she never seemed to make much progress. She sounded like a good match for Jordan Campo.

"You know, that explains something," Gail said. "I've noticed that Jordan comes in on a weird sort of schedule. Sometimes he's here early in the morning, and sometimes not until late afternoon. That's probably because he has college classes." She pursed her lips. "Come to think of it, he hasn't been around for a few days. You think maybe he went on a spur of the minute vacation?"

"I can't imagine he'd leave the cat high and dry like that." I looked out the front window to where Rochester sat at attention, waiting for my return – and his treat. "You have any dog biscuits today?"

"I do. I'm experimenting with a new recipe, one that uses beef-flavored baby food. You'll have to tell me what Rochester thinks."

She used a pair of tongs to pull a biscuit out of the case and put it in a paper bag. "I'm sure he'll love it," I said. "He is my baby, which means he gets a lot of treats."

That reminded me of Jordan Campo and his pampered pussycat. I paid for the coffee and the biscuit and carried them both outside. While Rochester chewed noisily, spilling crumbs on the sidewalk, I thought about what might have happened to Jordan. Was he on the run from someone else he'd tried to scam? Dead? Or had he simply spaced out?

I came up with no good ideas, and finally finished my coffee and began to walk back home with Rochester. We passed the old Victorian, but there was no sign of activity inside and I didn't need to check in on Shere Khan, so we continued without stopping.

When we got home, I pulled the stepladder from the garage and propped it up in the second-floor hallway. With Rochester at my feet, watching intently, I climbed up, pushed aside the access panel for the attic, and felt around for my other laptop computer.

The computer had once belonged to my next-door neighbor,

Caroline Kelly, who was Rochester's original owner. After she was murdered, I installed a set of illegal hacking tools on her laptop and used them to trace her life. With the help of the big golden, I was able to direct Rick to her killer.

Since then, I'd used those tools occasionally to help Rick when there were clues to be found online, in protected places that conscientious police officer couldn't go. This was one of those times, I thought, as I stepped down the ladder with the laptop in one hand. I was sure that Jordan's disappearance was linked to the spam emails he was sending, and that meant I needed to hack into his email account and see where the trail led me.

I set up the laptop on the butcher-block kitchen table. I didn't know enough about Jordan or his life to guess at his email password, so instead I opened a password-cracker program and plugged in the few pieces of information I could find – his birthday, his cat's name, and so on.

The software would generate potential passwords based on that information, and then go on to more random choices until it finally broke into Jordan's account. That could take hours, maybe even days, but it had never failed me.

Lili came in while I was sitting at the kitchen table watching the software work. I could tell she recognized the battered old laptop and had an idea what I was doing. "What's up?" she asked.

She sat on the other side of the table, and Rochester came over to nose her.

I told her about the cat and the spammer.

"If he loves the cat as much as you say, there's no way he'd have left her alone for so long," she said. "You think you can find him?"

"I don't know. Missing persons are out of my range of expertise. But I'm going to give it a try."

"Could he be dead?"

I shrugged. "It's a possibility. But Rick said there haven't been any unidentified bodies in town lately."

She snorted. "Lately."

"I do think he's in trouble. And I kind of feel like I need to help him."

"Because he tried to scam you?"

Was I just interested in revenge? Well, a little. I wanted to show Jordan who was the better computer geek. But there was more.

"People helped me when I was in trouble," I said, feeling my way through the ideas percolating in my brain. "I see myself in him, at least a little bit. You know, using some skills without realizing how deep I was getting in. And yeah, I admit, I want to show I'm smarter than he is. Don't try to scam a scammer."

"You were never a scammer. You did what you did because you thought it was right."

"That's what I always tell myself."

I'd gotten in trouble when my wife at the time suffered a second miscarriage. After the first, she'd engaged in a thousands of dollars of retail therapy which had nearly bankrupted us, and to prevent a recurrence I'd hacked into the three major credit bureaus and put flags on her accounts to prevent her from making big charges.

Because I could.

And because it was easier than confronting the pain we both felt. Unfortunately, I'd gotten caught, and convicted, and sent to prison. My marriage, which was already on shaky ground, had ended, and once I was paroled I'd returned to Stewart's Crossing to start over again.

My hubris had cost me a lot. I hoped there was a way I could help Jordan Campo, if he was still alive, see the error of his ways and use his talents for something more legitimate.

It wasn't until Sunday afternoon that the password cracker software dinged to let me know that it had broken into Jordan's email account. I poured myself a big glass of ice water and sat down at the laptop, flexing my fingers and feeling that old thrill rush through me. I was pretty sure that Jordan felt something similar if someone responded to his bitcoin spam.

No messages had been sent from his account for four days by then, though his inbox was flooded with messages from failure daemons and the regular detritus of anyone's account – offers to enlarge his penis, to lower his cholesterol, to vacation at insider prices or subscribe to magazines at big discounts.

Amongst all the garbage, I found a number of personal messages. His mother wanted to know why he wasn't returning her phone calls. "I'm worried about you, sweetie," she wrote. "Please call me."

Further evidence that he'd dropped off the face of the earth. I wondered if I should contact her and ask her to report Jordan's disappearance to the police, so that Rick could investigate. But how would I explain that I'd found her? Oh, by the way, I broke into your son's house to feed his cat and then hacked into his email account.

Not a conversation I wanted to have.

I kept reading. One of his classmates had emailed with information on what he'd missed in his comparative operating systems class and remind him they had a group project to work on.

Maybe I could approach the professor? Or Jordan's classmate? I put those ideas aside and kept reading. I finally found someone who'd fallen for Jordan's scheme, and I read through a couple of messages where Jordan, under his GrayMarketGary ID, corresponded with his victim, who signed his emails as Leo and used an email account called letthelionroar@gmail.com.

It appeared that Jordan went into Leo's bitcoin account and cleaned it out, and Leo began sending increasingly threatening emails, demanding the money back. "You don't know who you're messing with, bro," the last message in the chain read. "I will hunt you down and seriously hurt you."

Well, that was a smoking gun if I'd ever seen one.

It appeared that Jordan had ignored that message, dated four days before, along with all the other demands. I kept reading but there were no more clues in the email chain. I tried Googling Leo's email address, and the prefix he used, hoping he might have used the same one on social media, but came up with nothing there, too.

I was staring ahead in frustration when Rochester came up to me, his big plumy tail wagging. In his enthusiasm, he knocked over a picture Lili had left on the coffee table.

Fortunately the glass didn't break. I picked it up and looked at it. It was one Lili had taken with the camera in her cell phone, a photo of Rochester caught in mid-leap. I loved that picture, and I'd posted it to my Facebook account.

I scratched Rochester under his chin as I looked at the picture. Did Jordan have any other social media accounts, where I might find other clues? Maybe he was on Instagram or Pinterest.

I got Rochester a biscuit from the kitchen, told him he was a good boy, and then got busy online. Eventually I found that Jordan had an Instagram account. Most of the photos were of his cat—sleeping, playing with a toy, sprawled on its back waiting for a belly rub. The most recent photo, however, was the one that interested me.

It was an image of a pile of gold coins with the distinctive bitcoin logo, spikes from the top and bottom of the B so that it looked like a modified dollar sign. In the caption Jordan had written "i am king of bitcoin! just scored big from clueless cat."

I figured he was bragging about his theft of the bitcoins from Leo, aka letthelionroar. I wasn't that familiar with Instagram, so I Googled for instructions on viewing someone's followers. I followed the steps and saw a list of all those who were following Jordan – only about a dozen people.

One, however, was named Leonardo Campo.

Could he be Leo, the lion who was angry at Jordan? Why would Jordan scam someone in his own family? Did his Asperger's prevent him from understanding the social consequence? Not to mention that with his threats, Leo seemed pretty unhappy with Jordan.

Unlike Jordan, Leonardo Campo was very active on social media, posting pictures on Instagram and Facebook of himself out partying with lots of lovely ladies and good-times buddies. He and his pals were fond of Philadelphia Phillies T-shirts, gold chains, and backwards ball caps.

He didn't look like the kind of guy who'd be investing in bitcoins, though. He worked for a company that imported food from Italy, with an office on 9th Street in South Philly, which I recognized as being in the neighborhood of the Italian Market, where I'd often shopped when I was in the city.

Digging a little deeper, I discovered that he'd been indicted as part of a health insurance fraud scheme two years before, though the charges had been dropped due to some procedural errors.

It was time to call Rick again.

I established that he wasn't busy, and I could come over, though I'd be particularly welcome if I brought some beer with me. I detoured past the grocery in the center of Stewart's Crossing where I left Rochester in the car for a minute while I ran in and picked up a six-pack of Dogfish Head Firefly Ale, a bag of chips and a jar of salsa.

"What's so important?" Rick asked, as I walked in. Rochester charged past me to romp with Rascal as I followed Rick to the kitchen.

"I've been doing some digging on Jordan Campo," I said.

"You find him yet?"

"Nope. But I might have a lead on what happened to him."

Rick poured the salsa into a bowl and uncapped a couple of beers. I ripped open the bag of chips and we sat across from each other at the table in his kitchen. It hadn't been changed much since the house was built in the fifties; he'd put in a new fridge, oven and dishwasher, but the Formica cabinets were original, as was the big stainless steel sink and the brown and tan patterned linoleum floor. It was a comfortable room and I liked hanging out there.

I told him what I'd discovered about Leo Campo. "You think his cousin did something to him?" Rick asked, when I was finished.

"Maybe. You know anything about a big health care fraud case in Philly last year?" I explained that I'd found Leo among the list of defendants.

"That was a Mafia case, Steve," he said. "You're dabbling in dangerous waters."

"Which is why I coming to you."

He groaned. "What am I supposed to do with this information? Remember, we don't even have a missing person's report on Jordan Campo yet."

"Suppose I give you Jordan's mother's name and phone number. You call her up because you're investigating a possible email scam. I reported it to you, after all."

"And?"

"You see if she's been in contact with him. If she's worried, maybe you can get her to report he's missing."

"But I'm not investigating the scam."

"Sure you are. I reported it to you, right? You went to the suspect's home and found evidence that indicated he had disappeared."

"But what's the crime? Sending you the email?"

"I can give you the evidence that shows he stole from this guy."

He shook his head. "You ever heard of the doctrine 'fruit of the poisoned tree'? Means anything you acquired illegally can't be used in a court case."

"I can show you Jordan's Instagram account, where he put up that picture that indicates he stole from someone. That's out there in the public domain, right? You could just say that you were following up on my speculation and found evidence that Jordan might have committed a crime."

"This is all pretty sketchy," he said.

"At least bring it to your chief tomorrow." I held up my hand to tick off the points. "Local resident appears to be missing, because he left his front door open and his cherished cat alone without food or water."

A second finger. "Another resident provided you with information that indicates the missing man may be involved in criminal activity."

Third finger. "He may also have connections to the Philadelphia Mafia—because someone of the same last name, one of his social media connections, was arrested in a Mafia case last year."

I sat back. "That should at least give you enough reason to call his mother."

"All right. I'll give it a shot."

We ate some chips and salsa, drank our beers, and talked about a bunch of other things, and then I drove Rochester back home.

The next afternoon I was at work when Rick called. "I got a little leeway from the chief, and I called Campo's mother. She's really upset because he hasn't been in touch for nearly a week. And she agreed that he'd never leave the cat alone. She drove up from Philadelphia to pick up the cat and I met her at Campo's house. She confirmed that Leonardo Campo is Jordan's cousin, but she's divorced from the father and hasn't had anything to do with his family in years. She did say that she thought Leo's mother was connected to the Mafia, but nobody ever said anything specific."

Rochester sat up beside my desk. One of the reasons I'd taken the job I had, managing a conference center for Eastern College, was because I could bring the dog with me to work.

"So what are you going to do now?" I asked Rick.

"Start asking questions. See if I can get hold of the cousin."

"Be careful."

"This isn't my first time at the rodeo, Steve. I know the drill."

He hung up, but I wasn't satisfied. I didn't want my best friend getting into the middle of some Mafia investigation on my say-so.

I left work early and Rochester and I drove back to Stewart's Crossing, but instead of going straight home, I parked in the lot of the Wawa convenience store, a couple of blocks from Jordan Campo's house. It was still light, the sky a brilliant blue studded with puffy cumulous clouds. I hooked up Rochester's leash and we walked toward the old Victorian as the wind danced restlessly in the tops of the red, gold and orange maples and elms beside us, wafting down dead leaves in our path.

The front door of the Victorian was locked up, and Rick told me he'd passed the key over to Jordan's mother. So Rochester and I walked into the back yard. I hoped there would be a clue there that might indicate what had happened to Jordan.

The properties along this stretch of Main Street were narrow but deep, most of them stretching all the way back to the Delaware Canal. Rochester and I often walked on the towpath on the other side of the canal, but I'd never snooped into any of these yards.

We walked around behind the Victorian, where a rear entrance led to a staircase up to the apartments on the second floor. A single car was parked there, an old Toyota sedan. I pulled up my notes on my phone and ID'd the license plate as belonging to Jordan's car.

A screen of trees stood between the parking area and the river, and Rochester strained forward eagerly. I hoped that whoever lived on the second floor was out or wouldn't care that we were snooping around the yard.

As we walked toward the trees and the canal beyond, Rochester pulled and pulled and I worried that he'd picked up the scent of something – Jordan Campo's body? But he stopped at the base a small tree and began to sniff.

The lowest branch of the tree was broken, as if someone had pushed past it. I was examining the break to see if I could figure out how recent it was when Rochester sat on his hind legs and woofed once.

"What is it, boy?"

I looked down at the ground and saw the glint of something gold. Leaning down, I pushed away some dead leaves and found a thick gold chain on the ground, the clasp broken.

"Good boy," I said, scratching behind Rochester's ears. I picked up the heavy chain. How had it ended up back here? Had someone been fighting, perhaps Jordan and a captor, and the chain broke in the fracas?

I remembered the photos I'd seen of Leo Campo and all the gold chains he wore, and my pulse quickened. I scanned the area for more evidence of a fight, and I spotted some scuff marks in the dirt. It looked almost as if someone had been dragged along.

Once I had the gold chain in my pocket, Rochester was eager to move on. We followed the scuff marks as well as we could, my heart sinking. They led to the canal, where it was possible whoever was dragging Jordan could have tossed him in.

But then, a few feet from the water's edge, the trail changed direction. We followed, both of us with our eyes to the ground, and I didn't see the old warehouse ahead of us until we were almost there.

It was a small building, with a ruined dock behind it that had once accepted deliveries from a mule barge along the canal, a century or more before. The sign on the wall was old and faded and I had no idea if the building was still in use or not.

Except for what looked like a very new padlock on the door.

I figured that my experience had finally started making me act smarter. I called Rick and asked him to meet me there.

"Why?"

"Just an idea. Humor me, please?"

"I'll be there in five. Don't do anything stupid."

I agreed, and Rochester and I walked carefully around the perimeter of the building. It was a single story, with a peaked roof, no windows to peer into.

When Rick arrived, Rochester was eager to see him, jumping up to get petted. "Come for a walk with me," I said.

I showed Rick the scuff marks outside the warehouse door, and we followed the intermittent trail back to the yard behind the Victorian. I showed him the gold chain I'd found and explained what I thought had happened.

"Is this enough for you to get a search warrant?" I asked. "You have a missing guy, and a trail that leads from his yard to the warehouse."

"Probably. But I want you and the dog to go home. Don't get in any more trouble."

I was about to agree with him when a pickup on extra-big tires pulled into the driveway of the Victorian. With my hand tight on Rochester's leash, I followed Rick into the cover of the trees and watched as a big man got out.

"I think that's Leo Campo," I whispered to Rick. "I recognize him from his social media pictures."

Rochester sprawled at our feet as we watched Leo leave his car, carrying a bag of takeout food, and head down the path toward the warehouse. If he was taking burgers with him, then either Jordan was still alive, or Leo liked dining with the dead.

"I could tell you to stay here but I know you won't," Rick whispered to me. "Just be very quiet."

We stayed where we were until Leo was almost out of sight,

then hurried after him. We stopped beside a garden shed in the next yard and watched as Leo walked up to the warehouse and unlocked the padlock. He walked inside and shut the door behind him.

Rick called for police backup, and we waited outside the warehouse until a cruiser pulled up on Main Street and two uniformed officers joined us.

Rick walked up to the door and rapped loudly. "Police, Mr. Campo. Come out with your hands up."

We waited a couple of beats, and then suddenly the door burst open and Leo Campo came running out, low and hard like a linebacker. He knocked Rick over and sprinted past the two uniforms, who took off after him.

I rushed up to Rick and helped him up. "You OK?"

"Yeah. Let's see what's inside."

He kicked the door open wider and we walked inside. The room was dark, and I pulled out my phone and engaged the flashlight app.

Ahead of us, Jordan Campo was tied to a wooden chair with a long rope. One hand was free and he was eating a cheeseburger. He looked questioningly at us. "Where's Leo?"

"He's gone, Mr. Campo," Rick said. "Let me get you untied."

"Thanks. I really have to pee."

I sniffed the air, which smelled a lot like Jordan's house with the nasty cat litter box. "Rochester and I will wait outside," I said, tugging my dog with me. A couple of minutes later, Rick walked outside with Jordan, asking him questions.

He displayed the lack of affect I expected from someone with Asperger's, and I was glad it was up to Rick to question him and figure out what was going on. He admitted that he'd scammed his cousin out of about ten thousand dollars' worth of bitcoins. "Then he figured out it was me and came after me, wanting the coins back."

"What did you do?"

"I denied having them. He went off on this tirade, that the coins belonged to his boss, who was using them to move money around from overseas. He told me I would be in big trouble if his boss found out. Like I cared. Then he said his boss was this big Mafia guy, not someone I wanted to mess with. He left me here to stew around and maybe change my mind."

"You're coming with me," Rick said to Jordan.

"I have to get home to Shere Khan. She'll be missing me."

"Your mom took care of the cat. After you give me your statement we'll call her and get her to bring the cat back up here."

Rick looked at me. "I'll talk to you tomorrow."

I knew when I was being dismissed. I walked Rochester back to the Wawa parking lot, then drove home, where Lili was in the kitchen fixing dinner. "How was your day?" she asked, as I kissed her cheek.

"Interesting. Let me do something first, and then I'll tell you all about it."

I got the stepladder from the garage and carried it upstairs, opening the access panel in the ceiling and replacing the laptop with my hacking tools. As I did, I remembered a Chinese proverb I'd heard somewhere long before. "He who rides the tiger finds it difficult to dismount."

It was a good way of looking at my own habit, I thought. I had been riding the hacking tiger for years, and though I'd learned to temper my habit a bit, I was still finding it very hard to dismount completely. I hoped Jordan Campo would have better luck.

Story 4: Crime Dog on the Road

By the time we crossed the border into South Carolina from our home in Pennsylvania, my back ached from hunching over the wheel. My golden retriever Rochester was growing increasingly restless beside me, nosing me every few miles and trying to put his paw on the gear shift.

I gave up when I saw the faux Mexican signs for South of the Border. When I was a kid, my parents had taken me to a family wedding in Jacksonville, Florida, and we'd stopped at this complex of motels, restaurants and amusement rides. I guess I was always a sucker for kitsch – back then, I thought it was the coolest place ever. "When I grow up I want to live here," I had announced.

"And do what?" my father had demanded. "Be a waiter or sell tickets for rides? Not in this lifetime, kiddo."

I had pouted, but eventually my parents' plans for me had come to light—a college degree, a professional career. I think they'd be proud of how I'd been able to parlay my skills into my current management job at Eastern College – the main reason why I had three weeks' vacation at Christmas, and the time to drive Rochester to Florida instead of crating him for a plane ride or leaving him to board at the vet's.

We could use a break. Winter was sweeping into our hometown in Bucks County, outside Philadelphia, and we were recovering from a murder that had taken place in our gated community.

Rochester had a nose for crime—he had discovered a couple of dead bodies, and sniffed out clues to bring the perpetrators to justice. I was glad to get away from police and blood and danger.

My live-in love, Lili Weinstock, was a professor at Eastern, and the chair of the Fine Arts department. Her mother lived in Miami, and we'd agreed to travel down to see her. Lili had flown out the day before, and was already complaining about her mother's expectations of her, and even though she was in her forties and ought to have gotten over that kind of talk, Lili was eager for me to get to Florida.

I couldn't drive straight through, though. I looked over at Rochester and asked, "What do you think, puppy? You ready to stop for the night?",

He woofed once, a sound that came from deep in his sternum.

"I'll take that as a yes."

I got off I-95 and stopped at a shopping center parking lot to pull up the list of dog-friendly motels on my phone.

I chose the closest one, which turned out to be a single-story motor inn painted in vibrant shades of yellow, orange and blue. Rochester was delighted to jump out of the car, and immediately tugged me over to a bright blue chess queen sitting by herself at the side of the road, where he peed copiously.

Then we walked inside, and Rochester sat obediently by my side as I checked in. "Just one night?" the clerk asked. He was a young man with the right side of his head shaved, and I remembered my father's reaction when I said I had hoped to come back and live at South of the Border.

"Yup. On our way to Florida."

"You'll have lots of company on the road," he said. "I want to get down that way sometime myself. Take my girl, get us a room on one of those keys."

"We're only going as far as Miami. But I hear the keys are beautiful."

A Litter of Golden Mysteries

He got a faraway look in his eyes. "Yeah, that's the way I see them." Then he handed me the room card and said, "Enjoy your stay."

After I dragged our bags into the room, including all the ones that Lili didn't want to take on the plane with her, I took Rochester for a walk around the property. He fit the breed standard for a golden retriever to a T—he was friendly, intelligent and devoted. He had soft fur at the top of his head, smooth waves of gold along his back, and feathering along all four of his legs. His long, foofy tail often waved merrily, and I was delighted to show him off.

The area was crowded with moms, dads and small children, probably on their way to visit family for the Christmas holidays. They sat on the back of the giant papier-mâché models of elephants and whales and posed between the ten-foot tall chickens or by the legs of the ten-foot Mexican in his sombrero. A young guy in a backpack and camouflage pants rode the huge jackalope as if it was a stallion, waving his ball cap like a ten-gallon hat. People carried overflowing bags of fireworks and souvenirs from the gift shops.

Rochester stepped up to sniff the snout of a giant orange wiener dog with long black ears and I snapped a photo of him and sent it to Lili. Then I led Rochester over to a café with outdoor tables. It was sixty-eight degrees, according to the neon display by the street, but it felt almost tropical after frigid Pennsylvania.

Our server was a girl in her late teens with a pockmarked face. "I'll have the bacon burger with Swiss and a side of fries, and a root beer," I said. "And a plain hamburger for my friend here. No bun."

"Would your friend like a bowl of water to accompany his meal?" the girl said, and I couldn't tell if she was joking with me or just repeating a rote statement.

"That would be great," I said.

Rochester was fascinated by a little girl who wandered among the tables. She had blonde ringlets and wore an embroidered sweater with a cartoon character on the front, and miniature cargo pants with lots of pockets. I couldn't tell which table she belonged to; she seemed almost lost, and I worried that perhaps her family had gone off and forgotten her.

At a table across from ours, a drama began to unfold. The server delivered the check, and the man reached into his pocket for his wallet – which wasn't there. "I had it when we checked into the motel," he said.

"Are you sure you put it back in your pocket after that?" his wife asked.

"I know I did. And I would have felt it if it fell out."

"But when you sit, sometimes it rides up. I've noticed that. Look around the table. Maybe it fell on the floor."

He pushed his chair back and looked around. The little girl wandered past us and Rochester sat up on his hind legs and sniffed at her. "Can I pet your dog?" she asked, in an accent that was as deep South as they come.

"Sure. He's very friendly." She patted the top of his head, and he kept sniffing at her. I was surprised when he used his teeth to pry something out of her pocket—which fell to the ground.

"Hey, that's my wallet!" the man called. "That little girl picked my pocket!"

The girl knew she was busted, and she darted between tables until she reached the street, where she took off at a run. By the time the man had gotten up, retrieved his wallet, and looked through it, she was long gone.

"Is there a problem?"

The manager was a middle-aged blonde in a short-sleeved shirt with the restaurant's logo on the breast. The man explained about the wallet. "We've been havin' a problem with them gypsies," the manager said. "They start them out young, you know. Pickin' pockets and stealin' purses. You're lucky this dog helped you out."

The man thanked us, paid his bill and left. Only when we got ready to go did I discovered that the man had paid our check as well.

"You just can't resist sticking your nose into trouble," I said to Rochester as we walked back to our room. "I guess that's who you are. Can't get away from yourself, no matter how far you travel."

I reached down to scratch behind his ears, and he opened his mouth in a broad doggy grin. "My crime dog," I said fondly.

Story 5: For the Love of Dog

Part 1 – As White as Flour

As I read through my online news feeds I kept stumbling on deadly stories of love gone wrong. Was it the approach of Valentine's Day that led husbands to shoot wives, wives to stab husbands, and spurned lovers of all kinds to strike out at those who were supposed to be closest to their hearts?

I was lucky to have my loved ones close—Lili, sitting across from me at the dining room table, working on her laptop, and Rochester, sprawled at my feet.

"Take a look at this student portfolio." Lili swiveled her laptop around to face me. "The assignment was to take photos that represent a particular word, and she chose love."

Rochester recognized the word love, which I used on him all the time, and he sat up so that I could stroke the silky fur at the top of his head.

"The portfolio isn't sappy, is it?" I asked.

"Not at all. She went back to the ancient Greeks and their four words for love: *agápe*, *éros*, *philía*, and *storge*."

She pointed to the screen, a photo of a group of parishioners outside a church I recognized as St. Ignatius in Yardley, one town downriver from where we lived in Stewart's Crossing, a Philadelphia suburb. The word *agápe* was at the bottom of the photo, along with what I assumed was the same word in the

Greek alphabet. "I thought *agápe* was brotherly love," I said.

"It is, but it's also the love of God for man and the love of man for God," Lili said. She was the chair of the Fine Arts department at Eastern College, where I also worked, and she taught photography classes as well.

She flipped to the next photo, a collage of images of people kissing—a young man and woman, two elderly women, two thirty-something men among them. *Éros* was at the bottom.

"Romantic love," I said. Rochester had enough affection for the moment, and he slumped back down on the floor, resting on his side with his legs out.

"Exactly. A bit too politically correct—I think she could have used just one of the images. But she's a college student so I'll cut her some slack."

The next photo was what looked like a group of college students at a picnic. "Philia," Lili said, pointing to the word at the bottom. "Friendship, affectionate regard."

The kids were all laughing and engaging with each other, so I figured that was a good match. "And finally, *storge*." Lili pronounced the hard G with a light e at the end.

The photo showed a young woman sitting in a Morris chair at what looked like a coffee shop, breast-feeding an infant. The photographer had lit the photo so that the mother's dark skin glowed with an inner warmth.

"I can't say I've ever heard of *storge*," I said. "What does it mean?"

"I had to look it up myself. It means the affection between parents and children."

I nodded. "And again, a bit of political correctness. Breast-feeding in a public space. It's interesting the way she's managed to get across her opinions without hitting the viewer over the head. And the photos are all very well-composed."

"She has a good understanding of light and shadow, too." She turned the laptop back so it was facing her. "It's nice to get a student with real talent once in a while."

She went back to work and I thought about that word, *storge*. Family love. There was a time, not too long before, when I'd almost given up on ever experiencing that. When I was married, my wife suffered two miscarriages, and the emotional fallout from those experiences led, in the end, to the computer hacking event that sent me to prison for a year in California, and to our eventual divorce.

Then I had returned home to Stewart's Crossing, the small riverfront town where I grew up. I curled in on myself like those little caterpillars I often spotted on trees and tried to resign myself to single life. But within a couple of months, Rochester had come into my life, a strapping, enthusiastic golden retriever who wouldn't let me wallow in self-pity. His love had opened me up again so that when I met Lili, I was ready for her.

Since then, we had become our own family unit. After a stint as an adjunct English professor, then an employee in the alumni relations department, I'd been assigned to run a conference center for the college. Rochester came to work with me most days, and when the weather was temperate we often met Lili for lunch at a café on campus where we could sit outside, Rochester by our feet.

Those days were only a memory in bleak February, though. Valentine's Day was about a week away, and I'd already come up with the perfect gift for Lili – a covered travel cup in the shape of a wide-angle camera lens. She'd be able to use it to carry tea or coffee on the trek up to school, or have it on her desk as a reminder of her previous career as a globe-hopping photojournalist.

Rochester was even easier to shop for. I'd already bought a couple of hollow bones stuffed with peanut butter. With the addition of a few extra belly rubs, Rochester would be in puppy heaven.

He woke me the next morning at six-thirty to tramp through

the misty streets of River Bend, our gated community. The intermittent streetlights always reminded me of the one where Lucy met the faun Tumnus in the first of the Narnia books, glowing octagons atop iron poles, each with a horizontal arm our management company used to drape seasonal flags.

Each lamp was a halo of light, supplemented by security lights on townhouses and the occasional headlights of passing cars. We saw a miniature schnauzer named Robby whom Rochester liked, and after they sniffed each other, the dog's dad and I let them off their leashes for a romp through the shimmering dew.

By the time Rochester and I got home, the sun was beginning to rise in the east, splaying the streets with shafts of fuzzy gold light. I fed him and then hurried through a shower and got dressed, because we had an appointment that morning I knew Rochester would want to keep.

My friend Gail Dukowski, who ran the Chocolate Ear café in the center of town, had asked us to come down before she opened for a taste-test of new doggie treats she had created. The clothing shop next door to the café had closed, and with the help of her fiancé, she was going to turn it into a dog-friendly annex where humans and their canine companions could hang out together.

Because of food service laws, she couldn't serve both kinds of clients together, but the architect had put a door between the two rooms, and while bipeds were welcome to order food from the café, quadrupeds would have to stay on their side of the wall. Of course, a lot of people either had service dogs, or pretended that their dogs had a service function, but Rochester and I preferred to err on the side of the law. I was looking forward to the chance order my coffee and food and a biscuit for Rochester, and relax with him and my fellow cynophiles.

I left Lili dozing in bed and drove down into town with Rochester. It was about seven-thirty on a Saturday morning, and the rising sun glittered off the ice on the roads like knife blades. It had been a bitter winter, and I was longing for the first signs of spring, even though we'd have to wait at least a month for those.

As we drove down Main Street toward the café, I was surprised at how sluggishly traffic moved, until I finally saw a pair of police cars with flashing lights ahead of us, right in front of the Chocolate Ear.

I parked a block away and hustled Rochester out of the car, worried about what was going on at the café. Through the glass windows of the next-door space, where the renovation was taking shape, I saw my friend Rick Stemper, a police detective in Stewart's Crossing, speaking with Gail's fiancé Declan. Beyond them, a crime scene tech dusted the surfaces for fingerprints.

I assumed there had been a break-in overnight, and hoped the thieves hadn't gotten away with much. Rochester strained to go forward, but I held him back until Gail stepped out the side door of the café and motioned us forward. She was a slim blonde in her early thirties, and though she was twenty years younger than I was, we'd become friends when we both returned to Bucks County at around the same time. I loved the Chocolate Ear, and in warm weather I often spent time at the café tables that fronted on Main Street, Rochester by my side.

"What's going on?" I asked.

"It's terrible," she said, holding her arms against her chest. "You know I get up early to bake, right? Declan has been getting up at the same time to work in the new café before he has to leave for the office. This morning I told him, it's Saturday, stay in bed a while, but he wouldn't listen."

She started shaking, and I wrapped an arm around her shoulders. It was cold out there and she was wearing a light sweater, jeans and clogs. "Come on, let's get you inside," I said. We couldn't take Rochester into the kitchen so we climbed the stairs to the apartment above the café where Gail and Declan lived.

It was warm and cozy up there. Gail sat on the sofa in her living room and Rochester sat on the floor beside her, resting his head on her knee. She stroked his occiput, the back of his head, as I looked around.

The room reminded me a lot of the café downstairs. Gail had decorated it with similar Art Deco posters for French food products, and a glass-fronted case held her collection of antique baking implements, from wire whisks to cake pans in unusual shapes.

I sat across from her. "What happened this morning?" I asked.

"I was already in the kitchen when Dec went next door. He came back right away and his face was as white as flour. He said something like, 'that girl who cleans up, what's her name?' and I said that her name was Asya. And then he said, 'she's dead.'"

Part 2 – Hardy Boys

I was stunned. Though Stewart's Crossing looked like a picture-perfect small town, nestled against a crook of the Delaware River, I knew better than most that bad things happened anywhere.

"That's awful," I said, leaning toward Gail. "But how did she get inside before you opened for business?"

"We haven't cut an opening between the rooms yet, so the contractor we hired put one of those key holders that real estate agents use on the back door of the old dress shop," Gail said. "There's a code to open it up and it has the key inside in case the workmen get there before the boss does."

She rubbed her upper arms. "We called the police right away and an officer showed up a few minutes later. And then Rick came, and all these other officers, and they wanted to keep Dec there to talk to him." She wiped a tear away from the edge of her right eye. "You don't think they'll blame him, do you?"

"Rick's a good guy," I said. "If Declan had nothing to do with the girl's death, then Rick will figure that out. Did either of them give you any details?"

She shook her head. "Do you think Rick might tell you what happened?"

"I'll go downstairs and see. Rochester, you stay here with Aunt Gail."

He looked at me with sorrowful eyes, unhappy to be left out of anything, but he stayed by Gail's side and licked her hand.

I went back down the stairs, outside, and around to the front of the café. Declan was standing by the front window, and Rick stood behind him, talking on his cell phone. When Declan saw me he came outside. He was a tall, strapping New Zealander who'd come to the US for business school and then stayed on to be with Gail. He wore a heavy cable-knit sweater over jeans, and even so he looked cold, his face ruddy.

"I need to make sure Gail is okay," he said. "But the police won't let me leave."

"She's fine," I said. "She's upstairs with Rochester. What happened down here?"

"I came down around six because I wanted to sand a couple of the cabinets," he said. "We have a great contractor but the more work I can do, the cheaper it'll be in the end. I came in the back door and turned on the light, and I saw the girl's body on the floor."

His face was pale in the growing light, and his lower lip quivered.

"That must have been a shock," I said.

He nodded. "I went right over to her and I was going to feel for a pulse, but as soon as I touched her skin and realized how cold she was, I knew she had to be dead." He looked up at me. "She was wearing a T-shirt that read Toxic Womb. Is that a band, do you know?"

"Not a clue. Was there a lot of blood?"

"Yeah, around her head." I noticed that his hands shook as he spoke. "It looked like somebody bashed her head in."

"I'm sorry," I said. "I can see you're upset. Did you know her well?"

"I met her once or twice. She came in for a couple of hours after school to help with the clean-up, and I was usually at work then."

"After school?" I asked. "High school?"

He nodded. "She's seventeen, a senior at Pennsbury High. Her parents moved here last August from Philadelphia, and she wasn't happy about it. I think she was dating one of the carpenters, and that's how she got the job."

"Was she working yesterday?"

"I don't know. But before Gail and I went to bed I checked to make sure all the doors were locked, and there was no one inside."

"What time was that?"

He looked sheepish. "About nine o'clock," he said. "We get up so early, you know, so Gail can start baking."

"Hey, don't apologize to me for going to bed early. As soon as Rochester's finished with his late night walk Lili and I crash—and we'd go to sleep even earlier if not for him."

Rick stuck his head out the door of the space next door to the café. He and I had been acquaintances in high school, but when I returned to town we'd bonded over our bitter divorces. Since then, we'd become good friends, and both of us had moved on romantically. I had Lili, and he'd been dating a widow with a young son.

Rick and I were the same age, though his hair was grayer and thinner than mine. In his favor, he was in better shape, probably no heavier than he'd been in high school. He had a high-energy Australian shepherd, and he and Rascal ran every morning. Too bad Rochester was more of a meanderer than a runner.

"Levitan," he said to me. "You have an instinct that draws you out whenever there's a crime? And where's the death dog?"

"Rochester is not a death dog," I protested. "He's upstairs with Gail. We were invited to come by this morning to taste some of Gail's new biscuits."

"Well, she won't be baking anything for a while. This is a crime scene, and I don't need you or your nosy dog getting into trouble."

"So much for Joe Hardy," I said. "Big brother's in a bad mood today."

Rochester and I had helped Rick solve a number of crimes in town, and on a good day he considered me younger brother Joe Hardy to his Frank. Obviously this wasn't a good day.

He sighed. "No offense. But it's barely morning, I haven't had my coffee yet, and a teenaged girl is dead."

"I can get you a coffee," Declan said. "Cream and sugar?"

"Rick likes cappuccino," I said. "He probably needs a venti this morning."

"Coming up," Declan said. "You want one, too?"

I looked at Rick, who nodded slightly. "Sure," I said. "I'll take mine with mocha, though. And a shot of raspberry syrup if you don't mind."

"You might as well come in out of the cold," Rick said, and he opened the door wider for me.

It was chilly inside the unfinished storefront. The black and white tile floor had been installed, but the drywall needed to be skimmed and painted, and several of the cabinets Declan had mentioned sat in the middle of the room. A single table and two chairs were up against the wall, and Rick motioned me there.

"Bad morning, huh?" I asked.

"You got it. I was just getting ready for a run with Rascal when dispatch called me. He had to settle for doing his business in the back yard, which I'll have to clean up when I get home. Eventually."

"You don't think Declan had anything to do with this, do you?"

He shook his head. "Never say never, of course, but he says they were both in bed at nine o'clock, and before they took the body away the ME told me his best guess was that the girl was killed sometime between eleven PM and one in the morning, though the cold temperature might have slowed the decomposition."

"You know who she is?"

"She had a Pennsbury High ID card on her, and Declan confirmed that she worked part time on the construction crew."

"So what was she doing here at night?"

"That, my friend, is the question of the hour."

Declan brought the coffee in, and said he was going upstairs to Gail, unless we needed anything else.

"Can I help you with anything?" I asked Rick, after Declan was gone.

Rick sipped his coffee. "Oh, man, this is good. Actually you could help me."

I leaned forward. I was always eager to stick my nose into Rick's cases, though I rarely got to do it with an invitation.

"I get the delightful job of telling Asya Sharif's parents she's dead. And then I get to spend the rest of the day talking to anyone who knew her, and interviewing the guys who work for the contractor and checking their whereabouts." He sipped some more coffee as I waited for my assignment.

"You think you could pick up Rascal for me and keep him busy until I'm finished?" Rick asked.

Rick and I had long ago traded keys so we could look after each other's dogs if necessary. "Sure," I said, though I was disappointed that was all he needed. "I can head over there as soon as I get Rochester back from Gail. Maybe she'll even have a couple of treats for him."

I left Rick in the cold room with his hot coffee, as he began to make phone calls. I'd pick up Rascal and keep him with us until Rick was free. It wasn't as sexy as investigating a murder but after all, Rick was the cop. He had his job, and I had mine.

Part 3 – Angry Brush Strokes

Gail gave me a bag of doggie treats when I returned upstairs for Rochester, and I promised to keep track of which ones he liked best. By the time I made it back home with Rochester and Rascal, Lili had already gone out for a mani-pedi appointment with Rick's girlfriend Tamsen, who had become a friend of hers as well.

Lili had been keeping her car in the garage until a week before, when a cascade of boxes had tumbled over from their place along the wall while we were both out at work. She'd opened the garage door that night in the midst of a sleeting rain to discover there was no room for her to pull in.

She had not been happy.

I'd promised her I'd clean up over the weekend, and I was glad she'd gone out, because I hadn't been looking forward to her looking over my shoulder as I sorted through junk, asking if each item was really something we needed to keep.

I gave the dogs each a "pupcake," one of Gail's special turkey and sweet potato treats. They looked like human cupcakes with white frosting and a tiny carob-flavored bone on top. I tried to analyze how they enjoyed them but the treats were gone so fast all I could note was "gobbled."

Then I stuck one end of a tug-a-rope in Rochester's mouth and the other in Rascal's, and walked out to the garage. It was way too cold to work there, so I carried all the fallen debris from the center of the floor into the house. The torn boxes went into the recycling bin, and a bunch of books I'd forgotten I even owned went into a pile for the library's book sale.

Rochester and Rascal stopped chasing each other around the house periodically to check on me, but I wasn't doing anything that interested them, just filling a trash can with outdated faculty handbooks, student papers from the time I'd taught at Eastern, and an assemblage of newspaper articles and recipes I'd saved for unknown reasons.

A couple of the boxes had been packed up for me after my father passed away, when I was a guest of the California penal system. In one of them, I found a bunch of pictures that had hung in the bathrooms at my parents' house.

My mother believed that her bathrooms should be decorated with nautically themed art. A single sailboat at anchor in a New England harbor, a watercolor of the Florida Keys, and so on. Most of them looked like the generic compositions found back then at department stores. My mother was born in Trenton, across the Delaware from Stewart's Crossing, and kept shopping at various emporia from her youth until her cousin got mugged at a Shop Rite in a deteriorating neighborhood.

Indeed a couple of the pictures had labels from long-vanished mainstays of Trentonian commerce– Dunham's, Nevius Voorhees, even E.J. Korvettes. The final artwork in the stack was about the size of an eight by ten photo, though it was matted and placed in a much larger frame. The marking on the back read "From the studio of Everett Duplessis on the island of Barbados."

I vaguely remembered my parents had brought it home from a Caribbean cruise. Strong and almost angry brush strokes depicted a palm-lined coast and blue green water. The colors were rich and even the clouds had depth and dimension. At the center of the composition Duplessis had painted a dark-skinned man and woman, holding hands and bent forward, as if plowing through the storm together.

I assumed it was the kind of souvenir work mass produced for tourists, but when I Googled the artist I was surprised to discover a whole website devoted to his work.

A native of Barbados, he painted in what was called a "primitive" style, but his art had been offered in several galleries on the island. After his death, a dealer in New York had "discovered" him and was selling his pictures for big money. He was mostly a landscape artist, so work that included people was selling for a premium – especially ones like mine, which was part of a series he had painted depicting lovers facing various obstacles.

I took a photo with my phone and attached that to an email to the gallery that sponsored the website, asking if they would be interested in purchasing it. By the time Lili returned, I had managed to consolidate what had been in four large boxes into one, and fit it back into the complicated mosaic along the garage walls, making room for her car once more.

Rochester and Rascal dashed over to her as she took off her coat. "Hello, puppies," she said, letting them both sniff her. "No treats for you today." She looked up at me. "Is Rick here?"

"He asked me to look after Rascal because he caught a case this morning," I said. "A dead body at the Chocolate Ear."

"A dead body! Not anyone we know, I hope."

I shook my head. "A young woman who worked for the contractor. A girl, really, still a high school student."

She sat on the sofa, and both dogs settled at her feet. "That's so sad. Any time I see the death of a young person I think of the students we teach at Eastern. The world is so dangerous for them—for anyone, really. But students seem so vulnerable to me."

"They say the brain isn't fully formed until about age twenty-five," I said. "And the slowest parts to develop are the parts that control impulses and responses to temptation."

I sat beside her and took her hand, cool from the winter outside. "That part of my brain is a work in progress even though I'm long past twenty-five."

"I'd say your brain works just fine," Lili said. "So why aren't you and Rochester down at the café sniffing for clues?"

Lili knew that my smart golden and I had been able to help Rick with a few cases in the past. "I'm sure he'll ask for help eventually," I said. "While I waited for him to recognize that fact I cleaned the garage, so you can park inside now."

"You're a sweetheart," she said.

I reached over and picked up the Duplessis picture to show her. "I found this in one of the boxes from my parents' house. There might be some money in it. Not my taste at all, and if you don't like it and I can't sell it then I'll give it to the thrift shop."

We looked through the rest of the pictures together and she decided to keep a small one of a marina. "I think this is Greece," she said. "It reminds me of a place I lived for a while."

Every now and then Lil's history bubbled to the surface and I had to admit to a little jealousy—while she'd been roving the world I'd been stuck in a loveless marriage, and then incarcerated—which were pretty much the same thing to me.

Rick stopped by an hour later, and Rascal kept walking around him in circles, as if he was trying to herd his daddy back home. "All right, boy, we'll go in a minute," Rick said. "I need to ask your Uncle Steve a couple of questions first."

Here it comes, I thought. He needs my help.

"How well do you know Declan?" he asked. "I've met him a couple of times, always with Gail around, but I can't get a sense of him."

"Declan's a good guy. I kind of engineered his getting back together with Gail."

"Why am I not surprised?" Rick asked. He sat down on the sofa. "Tell me the whole story, Yenta. Isn't that Jewish for matchmaker?"

"Actually it's just a woman's name," I said. "She was the matchmaker in *Fiddler on the Roof*."

"Matchmaker, matchmaker, make me a match," Lili sang from the kitchen.

"Hey, no comments from the peanut gallery." I turned back to Rick. "He had a crush on Gail when he was in business school and she was dating his roommate. After he heard they'd broken up, he came to town looking for her. Rochester and I helped them realize they were right for each other."

"So the death dog is also a marriage counselor," Rick said. "A golden of many talents. But going back to Declan. You ever know him to be violent?"

"Not at all. He's the nicest guy."

Lili came into the living room with mugs of hot chocolate for all of us. "What about you?" Rick asked her. "You have an opinion of Declan?"

"He's handsome, if you like dimples in a man's cheek and that kind of broad-shouldered lumberjack build."

I was about as far from a lumberjack as you could get, and I didn't have any dimples.

"But he's way too young for me. He and Gail seem like a good match."

"So you don't think he'd cheat on her?"

Lili and I both said "No," at the same time.

"You don't suspect him, do you?" I asked.

"Just crossing my T's and dotting my I's," he said. "Gail's story jives with his. They went to bed around nine, woke up at five. He went downstairs, came back up right away."

"Then who do you think did it?"

"I spoke to the contractor, Bill Read, and each one of the guys who works for him. This guy Wafiq is the newest employee, been with them a couple of months. He's the girl's boyfriend."

He sipped his cocoa. "He says that he and Asya have been

meeting at the café late at night because that's the only time she can sneak away from her parents, who think she's too young to date. He says that he was going to meet her last night, but his truck wouldn't start and he couldn't figure out why. He texted her to say he wasn't coming but never got a response."

"Did she have her phone with her?" I asked.

"Nope. Which was weird, because what teenaged girl leaves the house without her phone?" He sat back against the sofa and stretched his legs. "This morning Wafiq had a friend come over and look at the truck, and he says someone stole the distributor cap. He took me out and opened the hood, and sure enough the cap is missing. But that doesn't mean he didn't remove it himself to give himself an alibi."

"Did you check his phone to see if he'd texted her?"

"Yup. She answered a text around seven, telling him she'd meet him. But then he tried her again three times after eleven, asking where she was, but no response."

"What did her parents have to say?"

"Honestly? They weren't as upset as I'd have expected. Her father said that she was a badly behaved girl, very disobedient. She watched TV programs they didn't approve of on her cell phone, and they caught her a couple of times taking her hijab off as soon as she left the house. They were planning to send her to relatives in Pakistan as soon as she graduated from high school."

"Did they know she was dating Wafiq?"

He nodded. "Apparently they moved out here from Philadelphia when they discovered she was dating him. He's a couple of years older than Asya and they don't like him."

"They didn't know she was still seeing him?"

"So they say. The father had no idea she was sneaking out at night, either."

"Wafiq sounds like a Muslim name. Was he from the wrong

sect or something?"

"Or something. You're right, he's a Muslim, and they met at some activity at the mosque in Philadelphia. But he's African-American and she was Pakistani."

"You'd think we'd be over all that nonsense by now," Lili said. "But there's so much division in the world. Even here in Stewart's Crossing."

"Bad things happen here, too, Lili," Rick said. "If they didn't, I wouldn't have a job."

My brain was racing forward. "Could it have been some stranger?" I asked. "Maybe someone saw her sneaking through town last night and followed her to the café. Was there any sign of sexual assault?"

Rick shook his head. "Just the blunt force trauma. We ran all the fingerprints we found and they all match either Gail, Declan, or one of the workers."

"Did you find the murder weapon?"

"Nope. ME says it was a hunk of wood, based on the fibers found in her wound. So it could have been something in the space, or something the killer brought with him."

He drained the last of his hot chocolate and stood up. "It's been a long day," he said. "Come on, you Rascal. Let's go home and get some chow."

The Aussie hopped up and began dancing around Rick again. After they left, I carried the dirty mugs into the kitchen, where I saw the Duplessis painting up against the wall. So much anger in his brush strokes, I thought. So much anger in the world.

Part 4 – Crossed Wires

Lili went upstairs to read after dinner, and I opened my laptop on the dining room table. I knew that my curiosity about Asya Sharif was morbid, and that it wasn't any of my business to snoop around, but I couldn't help myself.

I started at Facebook, where I found a surprising number of women by that name, but I found the one who went to Pennsbury High.

She wasn't very pretty; she had a bad case of acne and a moon-shaped face under a drab-colored Muslim head scarf. From the couple of pictures of her with her friends, I could see she was about five-four, and she wore cheap-looking jeans and long-sleeved sweaters. An innocuous-looking girl. Who would want to kill her?

She'd never changed her status to "in a relationship" even though she was dating Wafiq. All her friends were other girls, almost all of them from Philadelphia. She "liked" the Al-Aqsa Islamic Society and Kensington High School for the Creative Arts. She didn't write well in English, at least in her posts—they were riddled with grammatical errors and lack of capitalization.

In those she complained about what a small town Stewart's Crossing was. The same complaints I'd had when I was her age – the limited entertainment options for kids, the need for a car to get around, and of course about her parents, who were so old-fashioned.

At seventeen, I had felt trapped just as Asya did. Many of my high school friends lived too far away to walk or cycle to, and my parents monitored my homework and made sure they always knew where I was, who I was with, and when I'd be home. Now I realize they did all that because they cared about me, but back then I resented every restriction.

At least I'd had the lure of college ahead of me, a way out of Stewart's Crossing and into the wider world. Even so, I was scared of being on my own in a big city, and when I was recruited by the director of admissions at Eastern, and offered a scholarship there, I'd considered it the best option. It was close enough to

Stewart's Crossing that if I got homesick I could call my dad to pick me up for the weekend, but more cosmopolitan than my hometown because of the diverse student body. I could walk anywhere on campus or in town, and that made me feel freer than I had at home.

For Asya, the future held more circumscriptions—the third world atmosphere of Pakistan, further limits imposed by family and religion. Would her parents have tried to force her into an arranged marriage?

I didn't realize I'd been so sheltered by my parents until I got to college. Back then, the only alcohol I'd ever consumed had been in their presence, drinks like a brandy Alexander which had so little booze it was more like a dessert than a potent potable. I'd never smoked dope, had sex, or roamed the streets on my own after midnight.

The boyfriend had told Rick he and Asya often met at the construction site under cover of darkness. Was it bad luck that her boyfriend hadn't been able to meet her that night, and protect her from whoever attacked her? Or was he lying to Rick about the distributor cap? It was easy enough to remove the cap and send a couple of texts to establish an alibi.

I wondered if he had an online presence that might provide some insight into their relationship. Maybe she wanted to break up with him, and he wouldn't let her go. Maybe they argued over Muslim theology. Or it could have been simple jealousy, if she'd looked the wrong way at one of his coworkers.

Rick had mentioned his name, but I had no idea how to spell it. So I started with Bill Read, the contractor Gail and Declan hired, who operated under the business name We Nail It Contractors. I did a search for that company name, and came up with a couple of posts from homeowners complimenting the work that had been done.

One mentioned the workers by name—including carpenters Jerry, Scott, Evan and Wafeek. Nobody on Facebook by that name, though, so I switched over to Google, which generously told me that it had found results for Wafiq, and gave me a link to click if I really wanted to search for Wafeek.

"Thanks, Google," I said.

I went back to Facebook and came up with a hundred results for Wafiq, mostly from one guy's posts. But buried amidst the photos of climbing a mountain in the Philippines and a dessert bar in Alexandria, Egypt, I found a page for a young man named Wafiq Johnson. He currently lived in Levittown, Pennsylvania, and was a fan of the Al-Aqsa Islamic Society. And he was black. Bingo.

But that was all I could find. No pictures of him with other girls. No angry screeds about unfaithful girlfriends.

Did he have a police record? How could I find that out without asking Rick?

My hands hovered over the keyboard as Rochester rolled over on the floor beside me, whimpering and churning his legs. "What's the matter, boy?" I sat on the floor beside him. "Having a bad dream?"

He woke up and looked at me with his big brown eyes, and I felt my heart overflowing with love. Why was I screwing around online, snooping into something that wasn't my business, when I had a dog I could be playing with instead?

I scratched his belly for a minute or two and then he got up and stepped over me, then trotted off toward the kitchen.

"What am I, chopped liver?" I called after him, but he didn't stop.

I stood up. Well, if Rochester couldn't help me, maybe there'd be someone in my online hacker support group who could.

I had joined the group soon after returning home from California, at the strong suggestion of my parole officer. He thought it would be good for me to have an outlet for my frustrations over the restrictions that limited my computer use. Since then, I'd come to think of a few of the regulars as friends, and we'd shared a lot of small successes and difficult moments together.

Most of our interaction was through message board posts or emails, and I was surprised to see Ilovekitkat hanging out in the chat room, because usually our schedules didn't mesh well unless we made specific plans to meet online.

I typed **hello kitty** – just because I liked to play around with him. He was a teenager who'd been caught hacking into his high school's main frame. Like me, he wasn't malicious; he hadn't changed grades or anything, just left snarky email messages for his teachers and the staff.

yo mr cross wazzup?

My online handle was CrossedWires, a nod to both the wired internet and Stewart's Crossing. Ilovekitkat and I had bonded, though I was old enough to be his father, because we both had that insatiable curiosity that led us into places we shouldn't be.

Been snooping around in something not my business.

's tough. i know u r a control freak like me

Huh? Control freak? That wasn't me at all. But before I could process that, he'd moved on.

i tell you i have girlfriend now? @ school

High school?

no dude, got my ged last yr, going to college, this chick is in my intro mass comm class an aspie

I was having trouble keeping up with the way his brain ping-ponged around from subject to subject, and for a recovering English teacher like me it was hard not to criticize him for his lack of capitalization or punctuation. It took me a minute to realize that an aspie was someone with Asperger's Syndrome, but by then he had moved on.

> u know i cant concentrate in class so my therapist said to record lectures and listen later, stop & start when i want, this aspie chick already had permission 2 record so prof said i should talk 2 her.

Well, at least I could follow that. I knew his ADD, topped off with a helping of hyperactivity, had caused a lot of his problems in high school. He was only calm when he was lost in his computer, coding or hacking.

> so we got 2 gether 2 listen and she started making out with me dude i never had a girl go after me before it was awesome

I could imagine. I'd never seen a photo of Ilovekitkat, but I figured he was a typical teenaged geek, probably overweight, no social skills. My great-aunt Ida used to say, "Every pot has its lid." Good for Ilovekitkat that he'd found her.

> Gotta go we r meeting 4 pizza

The system displayed an automated message: **Ilovekitkat** has left the chat room.

Great. All we'd done was talk about him and his girlfriend. What about my problems? Did I have the same level of impulse control as Ilovekitkat and his girlfriend? I was supposed to be an adult. I owned a house, had a girlfriend and a dog and a job. Why did I keep sabotaging all that?

Rochester came over and rested his head on my thigh, dripping cold water on my pant leg. As long as I kept in mind what I had to lose, I thought I could control myself. Every time I got the impulse to hack, I had to think of Lili and Rochester. I hoped Ilovekitkat could get the same support from his girlfriend.

A Litter of Golden Mysteries

Part 5 – Ethnic Fix

After I fed and walked Rochester on Sunday morning, I left Lili asleep and took the big dog with me to pick up something for breakfast. I parked about a half-block from The Chocolate Ear and then hurried up Main Street on foot as the February chill tried to sneak its way in through the seams of my coat.

I was surprised to find the front door of the café locked and the dark green curtains pulled closed behind the multi-paned windows. A sign on the door had been hand-written on a piece of pale yellow stationery with the outline of the Eiffel Tower to the left. "Closed due to emergency. Will reopen Monday morning. Sorry for the inconvenience."

That was Gail. Even a simple sign had a French touch.

Rochester stopped to sniff the base of a tree as I peered through the floor-to-ceiling windows of the space beside the café, looking for evidence of the previous day's violent assault. Someone had scrubbed the floor, because there was no sign of blood. The cabinets were still stacked in the center of the room, that single table and two chairs by the side wall.

I tried to envision the area around the café at night. A few years before, Stewart's Crossing had installed Victorian-style streetlights along Main Street, and the closest one stood just a few feet away. If I was sneaking around, I thought, I wouldn't walk down Main Street, especially if I was headed toward the back door of the café.

Rochester sniffed at the front door, confused as to why I wasn't going inside. "Sorry, boy, café is closed," I said. "We'll have to go somewhere else. But let's look around first."

Gail rented the café, and her apartment above it, from a local man who owned the building. There were four storefronts on the ground floor: a chiropractor's office, a cell phone store, the former clothing store, and The Chocolate Ear.

The doctor's office butted directly up against an old stone

building that had once housed a bank but now was an upscale jewelry store called The Vault. But there was a gap between the Chocolate Ear and the post office, and Rochester began tugging at his leash to lead me through it.

I trailed along behind him to the back of the building and the small parking lot there, big enough for a handful of cars. Declan's SUV and the station wagon Gail used for deliveries were the only vehicles there. Rochester was very interested in the drainpipe by the side of the building, and I let him sniff there while I surveyed the property.

Five wooden doors faced the parking lot. The day before, I'd been through the closest one to me, a dark green portal that opened onto the narrow stairwell up to Gail's apartment. The door beside it had a sign in French script that read "The Chocolate Ear Deliveries," and I knew it led directly into Gail's kitchen.

The door I was interested in, though, was the one in the very center, which led into the rear of the space Gail was renovating. As Declan had described, it had a real estate agent's lockbox on it, and I assumed the key was inside the box, which was accessed by a combination lock.

I walked up close and peered at the frame. No marks indicating someone had tried to break in, no scratches or evidence of a pry bar. Whoever had gone into that room with Asya had either been with her, or followed her in while the door was unlocked.

Rochester tugged his leash and I turned around to face Canal Street, the narrow one-way alley that paralleled Main. It was mostly used by people who lived in the houses fronting the canal there, and those seeking access to the parking lots behind Main Street shops.

There was no light back there, and I thought Asya might have walked along Canal Street to avoid notice. It wouldn't have been hard for some stranger to have followed Asya through the darkened back streets, accosting her when she reached her destination.

A Litter of Golden Mysteries

Rick had said there were no fingerprints beyond those of the people who worked there, but it was a cold night, so not unusual for Asya's attacker to have worn gloves. Because I'd helped another inmate in prison with his appeal, I'd learned a lot about fingerprint science. There were two types: visible and latent.

Visible prints were formed when blood, dirt, ink or some other liquid was transferred from a finger or thumb to a surface. The kind of surface didn't matter much—it could be rough or smooth, porous or not. You could leave visible prints on anything from paper to cloth, metal or glass.

Latent prints were not so easy to see. They were formed when sweat or the body's natural oils were deposited onto another surface, and an investigator had to use powder or other means to detect them. It was harder to leave such prints on rough, non-porous surfaces, and in dry cold, as we'd had for a few days, it was even less likely that prints would take.

I closed my eyes and envisioned the scene in my head. Asya arrived at the back door, followed by an unknown assailant. She punched in the code and retrieved the key and unlocked the door. If she hadn't read Wafiq's text, she didn't know he wasn't coming and she might have left the door open for him.

The assailant could have made his move then, as she walked into the empty room. Perhaps he tackled her, preparing for a sexual assault, and she fought back. He might have grabbed a piece of wood and hit her, trying to subdue her, and then fled after realizing how much damage he'd done.

I was shivering, and not just from the cold. It was silly of me to be standing there in the February chill imagining terrible things. The fact of Asya's murder was awful enough.

Rochester was eagerly sniffing something on the ground, and I reached down for it. It was a tiny LED flashlight, the kind that can slip easily into a pocket. Or out of it, I thought.

It was about four inches long, but there was enough room for "Crossing Pack and Ship" to be printed on the barrel.

Was it a clue? Had the murderer dropped it in his hurry to leave the scene? Or just a random piece of urban debris? I'd have to show it to Rick and let him decide. Fortunately I was wearing gloves, so I hadn't put my prints on it.

I reached into the pocket of my coat for the roll of plastic bags I used to pick up after Rochester, and I slipped the flashlight into one of them.

By then, the big golden was ready to leave, and he tugged me back out to Main Street. With The Chocolate Ear closed, the bagel shop in Newtown was my best choice. I loaded Rochester into the car and headed inland.

My dad had this thing about bagels. He insisted that good bagels had to come from a place with a man's name above the door – preferably a Jewish name, but he didn't discriminate. When I was a kid we went to Abe's Bagels in Philadelphia, or Irv's Bagels in Brooklyn. Frozen bagels were an abomination. And the only real flavors were egg, onion and garlic, though I was allowed to order one rolled in kosher salt because I was a picky eater.

When an upscale chain opened in Princeton a few years before he died, I'd taken him there for lunch on one of my visits. He turned up his nose at the name – Old Nassau Bagels—and at most of the varieties, from sun-dried tomato to asiago cheese to chocolate chip. The bagels were too cakey for him, and he suspected they were made in some corporate kitchen and shipped in. "You can't beat an old Jew in a sweaty kitchen rolling dough out by hand," he'd said.

I was happy to avoid sweat on my bagels and I didn't care if the bagel-maker had had a bar mitzvah, but I'd gone along with him. And now that I was getting older I found his old habits popping up in me, which had led me to Moe's Bagels. I left Rochester in the car with the window cracked and joined a long line of my people waiting for their ethnic fix.

I saw more yarmulkes and tzitzit on men than I had in one place since my last trip to Brooklyn, and heard chatter in Hebrew that reminded me of those long dull afternoons studying the language in preparation for my bar mitzvah. Awash in nostalgia, I was surprised when I was next in line. I ordered a mixed dozen in two bags, keeping the garlic ones separate because Lili believed in segregation of baked goods of different flavors.

Rochester was eager to nose his way into the bag, and I had to break off a corner of one of the plain bagels for him to chew on. As I drove, I wondered again about Asya Sharif's murder. Had it been a random assailant? Or had someone deliberately set out to kill her?

What kind of deadly motive could an unattractive teenaged girl in the suburbs incite? I doubted she'd been some kind of Jezebel, stealing other girls' boyfriends. Or was another girl jealous of her relationship with Wafiq?

I had no ideas by the time I got home. I found Lili in the kitchen amidst the sharp, sweet smell of Cuban coffee. "Please tell me you brought us something delicious from The Chocolate Ear," she said, as I kissed her cheek. "Chocolate croissants? Those circular raisin snail things?"

"Gail's closed," I said. "You'll have to settle for bagels." I handed her the non-garlic bag. "Oh, there's one in there that Rochester started. He'll want to finish it."

"Of course he will," Lili said, as I handed her the cream cheese, plates, knives and napkins. "You know, Gail must be really upset to close the café. We should call her and see how she's doing."

"Why don't we invite her and Declan for dinner?" I asked, as I sat across from her.

Her face was a mask of horror. "Invite a gourmet chef for dinner at our house?"

"She's a pastry chef," I said, as I sliced a cinnamon-raisin bagel in half. "She probably doesn't do savory at all."

"I'm sure she learned everything in culinary school."

"And I'm sure she'd appreciate letting someone else cook for a change." I nodded toward her cell phone, on the table beside her. "Call her."

She did, and Gail said she and Declan would be happy to come, that they needed to get out of the house and would love to see us. She even promised to bring more treats for Rochester.

I was curious to know if she or Declan had heard anything more about the dead girl, but I'd have to wait. After breakfast I checked the newspapers online for any mention of her, but all I found was a tiny blurb in the Philadelphia *Inquirer* with no more details than I already knew.

Then I remembered the flashlight I'd found. I retrieved it from my pocket, leaving it in the plastic bag, and Googled Crossing Pack & Ship. I discovered it was a new operation at a shopping center on the outside of town.

I called Rick and made sure he was home, and told Lili Rochester and I were going over there. "I'll text you a grocery list," she said. "You can stop on your way home."

I kissed her goodbye and once again bundled up to go outside. The temperature had risen a few degrees with the sun, but it was cold. Rochester didn't mind; he was always eager to go for a walk or a ride in the car.

Rick met us at his front door as Rascal yipped and danced behind him. As soon as I let Rochester off his leash the two dogs dashed inside at top speed. Rick lived in the house where he'd grown up—after his parents had moved to a retirement community in Florida, he'd bought the place from them. His living room was warm and comfortable, though the carpet was a bit threadbare and the furniture was from the 1960s.

"What's up?" Rick asked as I took off my coat.

"I found this," I said. I handed him the plastic bag. "Or rather, Rochester did."

Rick groaned. "Don't tell me you were out sniffing around Gail's café today." He opened the bag and looked inside. "A flashlight?"

"Yup. I figure it was dark out behind the café on Friday night, and the murderer might have dropped it while running away."

"Where did Rochester find this?"

"A few feet from the back door. By that big maple tree alongside the parking lot."

"And of course you got your fingerprints on it."

I shook my head. "Gloves."

Keeping the flashlight in the bag, he peered at it. "Crossing Pack and Ship," he said. Then he looked up. "The killer didn't drop this. Asya did."

"How do you know that?"

"Because this is her father's business," he said. "I went out there yesterday to talk to him and his wife. I'll bet she had a couple of these, especially if she was sneaking around after dark."

I was disappointed. "So it's not evidence," I said.

"It's all part of the puzzle," he said. "You know that. I should get the ME's report tomorrow. Maybe there will be a clue there."

"I hope so. I didn't know her, but she was a human being and now she's dead. I want you to put whoever killed her behind bars."

"Believe me, I want the same thing."

Part 6 – Carpe Diem Moment

I stopped at the grocery on the way home and once again left Rochester in the car. I walked inside, following an old woman in a hijab like the one I'd seen Asya wearing in her Facebook pictures. Were they related? I shook my head. Surely there were more Muslims in Stewart's Crossing than just Asya and her family.

My mind kept drifting back to Asya as I shopped. Lili had organized her list by the aisles of the store, so I was able to get in and out quickly, but I noticed, perhaps for the first time, a whole section of foods for different cultures. A rack of Spanish seasonings beside matzo balls in broth, pita bread next to British marmalade. Curry paste, mango juice, and pumpkin seed kernels with a label that certified them as halal by the Islamic Food and Nutrition Council of America.

Back home, I helped Lili put together her mother's roast chicken with apples and onions, and while the chicken was in the oven, I went online again, looking for something sweet to supplement my Valentine's gift for her.

I looked down at Rochester beside me. "What do you think, boy? What would Mama Lili want for Valentine's Day?"

Lili wasn't too happy with the "Mama Lili" name, but she put up with it because I threatened to call her Mommy otherwise. "I did not give birth to that dog, so I am not his mommy," she had said, more than once. I knew she loved him, though, because I'd often find him curled up beside her on the bed, her hand resting on his golden fur, and I'd seen how often she laughed when he played with her.

What made her happy, besides Rochester and me? She had a real nostalgia for the Cuban foods of her childhood. During World War II, her Ashkenazi Jewish grandparents had left Poland and Russia and been unable to immigrate to the US, so they'd gone to Havana, where her parents had been born. They had met in college and married soon after Fidel Castro seized power.

Lili had been born there, and lived there until she was twelve, when her father had managed to get the family out. She loved all kinds of Cuban dishes, from that sweet, potent coffee to meat dishes like *ropa vieja*, and she could argue with any expat about the proper construction of a Cuban sandwich – whether or not to include salami, for example. She was strongly in the anti-salami camp, and whenever she visited her mother in Miami she came home with a bag of sandwiches to savor.

I wasn't going to order her a sandwich for Valentine's Day. Not even a dozen sandwiches. But was there some Cuban food I could find for her?

I ended up with a gift box of guava jelly, guava paste, and guava pastries, which came in a jute bag with a graphic of the island on it. I had no taste for guava myself—it was too sweet and gummy for me. But it would be the perfect gift for Lili.

Rochester dashed away from me and started barking. "Gail and Declan are here," Lili called from the kitchen. I opened the door for them, and a blast of cold air rushed into the living room. I kissed Gail on the cheek and shook Declan's hand, then took their coats.

"This was so nice of you to invite us," Gail said. "Everybody thinks that since I'm a chef I don't want to eat anyone else's cooking, but believe me, I'm happy to step away from the stove now and then."

"Well, you're in luck tonight, because Lili's roast chicken is awesome," I said. Gail went into the kitchen to see Lili, Rochester trailing behind her because he must have sniffed some treats in that bag she carried.

Declan and I sat in the living room. "How are you guys holding up?" I asked. "It must have been a pretty big shock."

"This was the second dead body I've seen, and I hope it's the last," Declan said. I loved the spiky rumble of his New Zealand accent. "At least I didn't throw up this time."

"When was the first?"

"My uncle has a sheep farm in Golden Bay, on the South Island," he said. "When I was sixteen I went up there to help with shearing. While I was there, one of the sheep kicked a shearer in the chest, and he keeled over almost immediately. The doc said it was a rare thing, but the hoof hit him at just the right place to stop the electric signal going to his heart."

"That's grim," I said.

"You bet. I never went back after that."

I was glad that Declan didn't ask how many dead bodies I'd seen because the list was gruesomely long, thanks to Rochester's nose for crime. Lili called us in for dinner then, and we sat down to an excellent meal. Rochester had learned that Lili and I didn't believe in feeding him from the table, so he sprawled on the floor beside me, hoping to get something when we cleaned up.

Gail had brought us a chocolate cake for dessert, and as we ate it, I couldn't help returning to the topic of the dead girl. "Did you ever talk to Asya?" I asked Gail.

"Just once or twice," she said. "She wasn't a very happy girl. Do you know, her parents didn't even know she was working there? She told them she was staying after school for club meetings."

"Because she was working with Wafiq?" I asked.

Gail nodded. "And because her parents didn't want her to have any money of her own. They figured that if they controlled the cash, they could control her."

"Not a good strategy," I said. "What about Wafiq? Either of you ever talk to him?"

"I had a couple of convos with him," Declan said. "I took a couple of days off to help out with the work." He looked down at the table, then back up. "I'm afraid he might have gotten mad at Asya and hit her. Not deliberately, you know. But he had a bad temper. He told me that's why he turned to Islam, to calm down and focus better."

"He wasn't born a Muslim?"

Declan shook his head. "His birth name was Tyrone, he said. He started going to this mosque in Philly, changed his name, got real religious. That's where he met Asya."

"I don't think he could have killed her," Gail said. "They were in love."

"Love might mean never having to say you're sorry, but it doesn't mean never hurting someone," Lili said. "Look back at all the crimes of passion through the centuries."

"I really believe people are good at heart, and that it's circumstances that make them act badly," Gail said. "I'm not saying I don't blame whoever killed Asya, or that he shouldn't be punished. But that kind of inner evil that you see in movies and horror novels? I don't agree with that."

We went on to a spirited discussion of the nature of good and evil. Declan and I did the dishes together, and as we were finishing, he pulled a small velvet box from his pocket and flipped it open. "I'm going to ask Gail to marry me on Valentine's Day," he said.

The diamond inside was round and big enough to look decent, surrounded by tiny green stones. "Those are emeralds," he said. "Gail's birthstone."

"Congratulations," I said. "I hope you guys will be very happy together."

He snapped the box shut and put it back in his pocket. "What about you and Lili? You guys going to tie the knot?"

"It's tougher to take the plunge after you've been divorced," I said. "Lili's been through the mill twice, me once. We're both happy with the way things are right now, but that doesn't mean we'll never get married."

I thought for a moment of Asya and Wafiq. They'd never have the chance to marry, if that had even been a possibility between them. It was one of those carpe diem moments—did I want life to get away from either of us before we'd made that commitment to each other?

It was something to consider.

Part 7 – The Four Types of Love

I was busy at work on Monday, and didn't have time to think about Asya Sharif and who might have killed her, which was a good thing. Late in the afternoon, I received an email back from the gallery in New York about the Duplessis painting. They were happy to offer me a couple of hundred bucks for it, along with some money for shipping, and I wrote right back to say that I accepted.

I stopped at The Chocolate Ear on my way home Monday so that Rochester could thank Gail in person for the treats she'd brought for him, and to tell her which ones he'd liked the best. Bill Read, the contractor, was the only one in the new space, and he let me and Rochester in. I poked my head through the door to the café and saw Gail alone behind the counter, just a couple of customers at tables. She looked harried and almost frightened.

"Can I leave Rochester here for a minute?" I asked Bill, and he agreed.

I stepped into the café and up to the counter. "What's the matter?" I asked.

"The police came today and arrested Wafiq," she said, in a low voice. "I asked Rick what evidence they had against him but he wouldn't say. I keep thinking about him working just next door. What if he'd gotten angry at me? Would I be the one he'd killed?"

"In the first place, we don't know that he killed Asya," I said. "That's for the police to figure out and the DA to prove. And you can't go through your life worrying that there's a murderer next door. You'd never go outside if you felt that way."

"It's okay for you to say. You're a guy, and you can take of yourself. Asya was just a teenaged girl."

"Where's Declan?"

"He had to work today, but he should be home soon. I've decided I'm going to close at four o'clock for the next few days because I don't like being here after dark."

"Would you like me to stick around until Declan gets back?"

"That's sweet of you to offer," she said. "But Bill's working next door and he already said he'll be here until then."

"Well, if you need anything, just call," I said. "I'm sorry I don't have much to report about those treats you gave Rochester. He ate every one of them as fast as he could, though he spit out the squares you said were flavored with blueberry and pumpkin."

"That's good to know," she said. A couple of elderly women in red hats came in then, and Gail got busy helping them. I picked up Rochester from Bill, and we walked down the street to the Stewart's Crossing police station. I walked into the lobby, keeping him on a short leash. I showed my driver's license to the officer behind the glass window and asked if Detective Stemper was there.

He made a call, then said, "He'll be out to get you."

Rochester had a love affair going with the desk sergeant, who always had some treats on hand for the K-9 officers. Once Rick came out to let us in, Rochester saw his friend and started jumping up and down with delight.

I left my dog happily chewing a biscuit and followed Rick across the room to his desk. "Let me guess," he said. "You heard we made an arrest in the girl's murder and you wanted to snoop around."

"Well, yeah," I said, as I sat down beside him.

"I got the autopsy results this morning," Rick said. "Asya was pregnant. Went back to see Wafiq and ask him about it but he says he didn't know."

"You think he's telling the truth?"

Rick shrugged. "I'm not sure Asya knew herself, but the DA decided to prosecute him because all the circumstantial evidence is there. Wafiq had access to the construction site, he had plans to meet her and no real alibi, and the other workmen said he had a bad temper. One of them said he'd seen Wafiq yelling at Asya a few days ago."

"And that's enough?"

"It's enough to put him in the lockup waiting for processing."

I didn't know Wafiq, and I hadn't known Asya, but I was sad about the way their love story had come to an end. As Rochester and I drove home, I thought again about the development of the brain, the way impulse control wasn't fully in place until twenty-five. How old was Wafiq? Had he really struck out at Asya?

It wasn't my business, I reminded myself. I sympathized with the whole impulse control thing, based on my own difficulties resisting the urge to hack, but I had to focus on my own life and those I loved. Gail was right to be worried; bad things happened all the time, and I didn't want anything to hurt Lili or Rochester, at least not if I could prevent it.

That night Rochester kept trying to help me as I packed up the Duplessis painting, getting underfoot as I retrieved an empty box from the recycle bin, the packing tape and a marker for the box.

"What's the problem, boy?" I asked. "Do you like this painting? Want to keep it?"

I held it up to him but he just went down on all fours and stared at me.

When I had the box all sealed up and ready to go, he jumped up and put his paws on the kitchen counter, knocking off his leash and the little flashlight I used when we walked after dark. That reminded me of the flashlight I'd found behind Gail's bakery, the one with the logo of the pack and ship place.

Tuesday morning Rochester was still bothered by the package that contained the Duplessis painting. "Fine? You want me to get that out of the house?" I asked him, as we were getting ready to drive up to Friar Lake. "Let me find the closest pack and ship place."

A new shopping center had opened a few weeks before along the River Road, on my way to work, and I was pleased to see that a shipping franchise had opened there. The center had a raw feel to it—the verges were still piled with dirt, with sprinkler hose sticking out like alien tentacles. One part of the lot hadn't been striped yet, and several of the storefronts were covered in brown paper.

I pulled up in front of Crossing Pack and Ship. The name was familiar to me, though I knew I'd never been there before. Then I saw a sign in the window that indicated Mr. Mohammed Sharif was a notary public, available to notarize documents for a small fee.

I remembered. Rick had told me he'd come out to the store to tell Asya's father about her death.

Rochester had knocked the flashlight over the night before—but was that just because he was eager for a walk? Or was he doing it to remind me of the one he'd pointed out to me in the Chocolate Ear parking lot?

I looked at him. "Did you want me to come over here, boy?"

He sat up on his hind legs and looked out the window. "I guess that's a yes." I lowered the window an inch and left him watching me as I walked up to the front door.

The store was neat and modern, with a rack of tape, boxes and other shipping supplies along one wall. A tall, distinguished-looking Arab man stood behind the counter, filling out a form for the customer in front of me. As he straightened up I saw he wore a name tag that read "Mo."

So he was Asya's father. I watched him as he finished with the customer in front of me, looking for any visible signs of sadness or mourning, but I saw none. Not that I was expecting any – Jews wore their losses openly, in black clothes and torn ribbons, but as far as I knew such displays were not a part of Islam.

I stepped up to the counter when I was my turn and placed the box with the painting inside on the scale. While Mo began typing information into his system, I noticed a tray full of those tiny flashlights on the counter, and remembered Rick noting that Asya had probably had a bunch of them. I picked one up and examined it.

"Please, take one," Mo said, in a clipped accent. "They just arrived on Friday afternoon. I am very satisfied with the way they came out."

Friday afternoon, I thought. Asya had been killed on Friday night, and from what Rick had said, I knew she had gone directly to the café after school, and hadn't gone to the store before leaving the house to meet Wafiq.

But her father could have taken some of the flashlights home and given them out.

"Would you mind if I took an extra one?" I asked. "I'd like to give one to my daughter to carry with her at night."

He blinked a couple of times and the edges of his mouth lowered into a frown. "Yes, most certainly," he said. "I meant to take some home for my own family on Friday night but forgot, though at least I remembered to take one for myself." He shook his head. "Unfortunately I lost it almost immediately. I suggest you put it on your keychain so it does not fall out of your pocket."

"I'll do that," I said. So he didn't give Asya one of the flashlights, and he'd lost the one he pulled out for himself.

Did that mean the one Rochester had found was his? And that he'd been at the café on Friday night?

"If you are happy with our service, please tell your friends," he said, bringing me back to the present. "It is difficult for a new business to get started, and we would love to have your recommendation."

"I'm happy to support local businesses." I handed him my credit card and paid for the shipment, and then walked out.

As soon as I was back in my car, I called Rick. "Did you ever talk to the father about that flashlight Rochester found behind the café?"

"Never had to. We arrested Wafiq, remember?"

"I think you should speak to him." I repeated what Sharif had told me, about the arrival of the flashlights, the way he'd lost the one he took for himself. "If it has his fingerprints on it, that will place him at the scene, right?"

I expected him to argue with me, to say that he already had a suspect in custody. "Her parents didn't seem surprised when I told them she had been killed," he said. "He said some stuff about her being with Allah now, hoping she would mend her evil ways. It didn't sound like something you'd say right after hearing your daughter was dead."

"Asya thought her parents didn't know she was sneaking out at night to meet Wafiq. But suppose he caught her going out, and he followed her to see where she was going."

"There's a big leap from following her to killing her," Rick said.

"He might not have meant to," I said. "Maybe he got angry and hit her, and she hit her head."

"That's not consistent with the ME's report." I heard him speak to someone nearby, and then he came back and said, "I have to go now. But I'll talk to the chief and see whether he wants me to go back and talk to the family again."

I drove to work after that, thinking about those different kinds of love Lili's student had photographed. What was the one for familial love? It was the weird-sounding one, the one I'd never heard of before.

I racked my brain until it coughed up the word *storgē*. It had such a positive connotation, but what happened when a family member disappointed you? Could you maintain the love, or would it curdle?

I thought back to those two babies my ex-wife had miscarried. My feelings toward them had been so complicated. I loved them, of course; they were a part of me. Mary and I had made them together, in an act of love.

But for a while after I went to prison, I blamed them for all that had happened. If the first baby had survived, Mary wouldn't have gone on the spending spree that nearly bankrupted us. And if the second had made it to term, I wouldn't have been tempted to hack into the credit bureaus in an attempt to protect both of us from more fiscal woes.

Eventually, with the help of the prison chaplain, I'd begun to take responsibility for my actions, and those feelings of *storge* had returned, colored with a deep sadness. By then I accepted that I would not father any more children, and that perhaps I might never have a family around me.

Rochester, and then Lili, had changed all that. Now I felt part of a family again, and that feeling of *storg* welled up in me. As I pulled into the parking lot at the conference center, I looked over at Rochester and felt myself start to tear up at the second chance I'd been given.

He leaned forward and licked my face, and I laughed.

Part 8 – Valentine's Day

Late that evening, Rick called as I was lounging in bed, Lili beside me, Rochester at my feet.

"Another triumph for Rochester the wonder dog," Rick said. "I went over to the Sharifs this evening to quiz the father about that flashlight, and he told me the same thing he told you—that he'd grabbed one from the box on Friday as he closed the store, but then lost it almost immediately."

"Did he realize why you were asking?"

"Didn't seem to. But Asya's mother must have figured it out, because she started to cry. She didn't cry at all when I told them she was dead, but she's crying about a flashlight? I thought that was weird so kept talking to her, drawing her out about Asya."

Rochester got up from the foot of the bed and clambered toward me, as if he wanted to hear what Rick was saying.

"Eventually she told me that she'd found a pregnancy test in the trash on Friday evening. That she and the father had confronted the girl and she admitted she was still seeing Wafiq."

"That couldn't have gone over well."

"Apparently not. The father sent her to her room and confiscated her phone. He saw a text from Wafiq confirming they were meeting at the café, and he texted Wafiq back to say yes. He drove over to Wafiq's house and took the distributor cap from his truck, then drove to the café to wait for Asya. He followed her in and confronted her."

"What did he say—was it an accident?"

"Nope. He was almost proud of killing her. He said that he did what Allah would have wanted. The girl was a blot on her family and her culture and needed to be eliminated." He sighed deeply. "Needless to say, I arrested him, and we let Wafiq go."

After I hung up, I turned to Lili. Rochester was snuggled in between us, and I stroked his head as I told her what Rick had said.

"That is just tragic," she said. "That any father could find a way to justify killing his own child."

I thought back to our conversation about how we both feared for Eastern students, because the world was such a dangerous place and young people were so vulnerable. "*Storge* only goes so far," I said. "But I'll be happy if it always stays here, between you, me and Rochester."

She leaned over the dog's bulk to kiss me, and he squirmed around so that he could lick both our faces.

The day before Valentine's Day, Gail texted me to say that she had some special treats at the café. I said I'd stop by on my way home from work.

February 14th dawned bright and sunny, as if Mother Nature was shining on lovers everywhere. I gave Rochester his peanut butter bones, and Lili her camera lens mug and the package of guava delicacies. She knew my weakness for chocolate, and she had a whole basket of treats for me, which I promised to share with her.

That evening I stopped at the café, assuming Gail had some more pupcakes for Rochester. She did, but she also had a heart-shaped chocolate cake, perfect for two, to give me. "Rick told me that you helped him find out that it was Asya's father who killed her," she said. "Declan and I wanted to say thank you."

I noticed that Gail was wearing the diamond and emerald engagement ring Declan had showed me. "So he asked you," I said, nodding toward it.

She beamed. "He did. And of course I said yes."

I congratulated her, and as I did I remembered those four types of love Lili's student had chronicled. I was sure that Gail's and Declan's wedding would cover *agápe*, *éros*, *philía*, and *storge*, and I told her that Lili and I would be delighted to celebrate with them however they wanted.

"For starters, the new room is going to be ready next week," she said. "You and Lili and Rochester will have to be there for our grand opening."

And grand I knew it would be, though tinged with loss. A darkness had fallen over that single room. But with lots of love, of all types, it could become a place of joy. I looked forward to being a part of that.

Story 6: Nectar of the Dogs

It was a beautiful spring Saturday in Bucks County, and I was feeling nostalgic for the neighborhood where I grew up, a few miles from the townhouse where I lived with my golden retriever, Rochester. I decided to take him for a walk around the lake behind my childhood home, so he could run along the grassy verge beside the water, and I could indulge in a few childhood memories.

I'd spent many summer days swimming in Silver Lake with friends, or rowing out to the middle of the lake and leaning back to look at the clouds and letting the boat drift as I daydreamed of the life I'd have when I got out of Stewart's Crossing.

Things hadn't worked out the way I'd hoped. But those experiences had led me to a life with Lili and Rochester, so I wasn't complaining.

I parked on the street by the access path between houses that led to down to the lake, and I let Rochester off his leash so he could sniff to his heart's content.

He spotted the female golden retriever down by the water at the same time she saw him, and they took off toward each other. It was beautiful to watch their lean bodies in flight and the way the sun-colored fur on their legs lifted in the breeze, but since I didn't know the other dog, or the woman with her, I went running after him, calling his name.

The two dogs collapsed into a love fest, the female rolling on her back so that Rochester could sniff her. "Sorry," I said to the woman as I got there. "I shouldn't have let him off his leash, but there's something about the first beautiful day of spring."

"I know," she said. "I bring Sophie over to see my parents and we always come for a walk along the lake."

I looked more closely at her. She was about my age, mid-forties, with dark hair cut in a pageboy. There was something familiar about her face, and it took me a moment to place her. "Diana?"

She looked at me.

"Steve Levitan." I pointed across the lake. "I grew up in that white house over there."

"Of course," she said, and we hugged. "Wow. How long has it been? High school, I guess."

I hadn't seen Diana Ryan since our Pennsbury High graduation, over twenty years before. Though there were a few strands of gray in her hair and some laugh lines around her eyes, she looked like the same girl I'd been in class with starting in kindergarten.

"You were Jerry Brown, weren't you?" she asked. "I was John Anderson."

It took me a moment to remember we'd done a mock presidential election in our social studies class, where various classmates had taken on the roles of candidates. "At least you made it to the final election," I said. "I was knocked out in the primaries."

Rochester and Sophie began to romp around together on the fresh grass, sprinkled with tiny yellow buttercups. "You still live in town?" I asked.

"Across the river in Pennington. I teach at the Cambridge School there. You?"

"After my mom died, my dad sold the house and bought a townhouse in River Bend, on the outskirts of town. I live there now. I run a conference center for Eastern College up in Leighville." I looked behind her, toward the house where she'd grown up. "Your parents never moved?"

She shook her head. "They could never agree on a place to go, and now it's too late. My dad's not doing well."

"I'm sorry to hear that."

We talked for a few more minutes, and then she called Sophie to her and they walked back along the edge of the lake toward her parents' house. Watching her go, I saw the tiny Cape Cod house where Edith Passis, my old piano teacher lived, across from the Ryans. I decided that as long as I was in the neighborhood, I'd stop by to see Edith.

She was a small woman with pink skin and a puffball of white hair. With both my parents dead, she was a connection to them, and to an earlier, more innocent time. Rochester and I came by to visit her every few months.

"Steve! How nice of you to stop by," she said, as she opened the door. "And Rochester, too. Come on in."

Edith's baby grand piano still took up most of the living room, and I remembered all the years I'd sat beside her on the hard bench, struggling to make sense of the notes on the sheet music and Edith's reminders about fingering and rhythm.

"I just baked some gingersnaps," Edith said as she led us into her kitchen. "Rochester can have one, can't he?"

"Ginger is safe for dogs, and Rochester loves gingerbread cookies. I'm sure he'll be delighted."

I settled into a high-backed Windsor chair at Edith's table, and Rochester sat on his haunches beside me, intensely interested in the plate of cookies Edith brought out. I broke off a piece and fed it to him, and he wolfed it down, then grinned at me pleading for more.

Edith joined us at the table with a pot of fresh-brewed tea, and as we sipped and ate—and I fed cookie bits to Rochester—I told her about running into Diana Ryan.

The Ryans were the first mixed marriage couple I knew. Mr. Ryan was Irish Catholic, and his wife Aphrodite was Greek Orthodox. The Ryans had arranged that their son would go to St. Ignatius in Yardley with his father each week, while Diana would go to St. George's in Trenton with her mother. It struck me then as an odd compromise.

Now a mix like that is commonplace, but back then it was the subject of gossip. "People said that Frank Ryan drank," Edith Passis said.

"And did he? Or did people just stay that because he was Irish?"

"A little of both, I think. In the seventies, of course, everyone served cocktails at home, and there was always a bottle of wine circulating. Frank drank Irish whiskey, neat, often with a beer chaser. Back then, you know, beer was considered very low class. None of the microbrew or flavored stuff. And women never drank it, of course."

She sighed. "Frank Ryan was a hard man, very set in his ways. You know he never approved of the man Diana married?"

"I didn't. Is there something wrong with him?"

"I've met him a few times, and he seems like a nice young man," Edith said. "Of course, he must be about your age, so you wouldn't consider him young. I believe Diana knew him when they were children, going to Greek school at St. George's in Trenton."

"Then why wouldn't Mr. Ryan like him?"

"From what I understood from Aphrodite, Frank felt that Diana betrayed him by marrying a Greek instead of a Catholic."

I'd had enough cookies, and so had Rochester, so I pushed the plate away and he settled beside me on Edith's tiled floor. "My parents wouldn't have been happy if I'd married a woman who wasn't Jewish," I said. "Though I doubt they'd shut me out for it."

"Your parents were lovely people," Edith said fondly. "Your mother was the mainstay of the Garden Club and she always had those beautiful hibiscus she raised on your porch to show off. And we wouldn't have done nearly so well with the dam repair if your father hadn't shepherded it through."

It was always good to hear Edith speak of my parents. They had both been civically minded, involved with all kinds of neighborhood activities, and my father had often used his engineering background when it came to improvement projects, like when the dam between the two lakes sprung a leak and the neighbors had to be assessed to pay for the repairs.

"Diana has a teenage daughter," Edith said, startling me out of my reverie. She must have surprised Rochester, too, because he sat up and nuzzled my leg. "Mary Elizabeth. She's autistic, you know."

"I didn't. That's sad."

"I've seen her only a couple of times, when Diana brought her over to see Aphrodite. She's not good with strangers, won't look you in the eye, and has these obsessions. But apparently she's very bright, with a scientific bent. The last time I saw her she was only interested in talking about her chemistry class."

For a brief moment I thought of those two babies that Mary had miscarried. What if one of them had survived, only to be diagnosed with something like autism? I hoped I'd love the child just as much, though I knew those issues had to make life more difficult.

Rochester woofed once, and I said, "I know someone who wants his dinner. I guess I ought to get him home."

"It was so nice of you to stop by." Edith reached her hand out to Rochester. He licked it eagerly and she smiled. "You enjoy your dinner, boy."

"He always does. Lately I've been dosing his meals with a glucosamine spray that the vet says will help his joints. He's going to be four years old soon, and I want to make sure he stays healthy for a long time."

"An excellent wish for all of us," Edith said. We stood up, and I kissed her goodbye, and then walked Rochester back around the lake to where I had parked.

I didn't think of Diana Ryan again until a few weeks later, when Edith called me to let me know that Frank Ryan had passed away, and to ask if I'd be able to drive her to the funeral, at St. Ignatius. It had rained the day before, and the roads were slick, so Edith wasn't comfortable driving on her own.

I was happy to oblige. I took the morning off from Friar Lake and picked up Edith under gray skies.

"Do we know what Frank Ryan died of?" I asked Edith as we drove down Main Street toward Yardley.

"Heart attack, or so I heard," Edith said. "But of course, when you get to our age that can be a mask for a whole lot of other conditions."

"How are you doing these days?" Arthritis had caused Edith to give up teaching piano lessons a few years before, and she'd had a variety of small health problems.

"The devil won't get me yet," she said, smiling.

I pulled into the parking lot beside a hedge of yellow forsythia that reminded me of those tiny buttercups I'd seen when I took Rochester over to the lake, and we'd seen Diana and her golden Sophie. I helped Edith out of the car and she took my arm as we walked up to the church.

Diana wore a knee-length black dress and black pumps as she stood in the church doorway greeting people. "Mrs. Passis," she said, as she leaned down to kiss Edith. "It's so kind of you to come."

She looked up at me then. "And Steve! We don't see each other for twenty years, and now twice in a month."

We hugged hello again, and then she stepped back. More people came in and Diana turned to them. I recognized Aphrodite Ryan, who looked very earth-mother in a flowing black dress and dangling earrings in the shape of curly-ended Greek crosses.

We hugged her, and then shook hands with Diana's husband George, her brother Cliff and a tall, cadaverously-thin man who introduced himself as "Nick, a friend of the family."

I slid into a pew beside Edith. "Isn't that odd, to have a 'friend of the family' up there in a receiving line?" I asked. "He can't be her boyfriend, can he? Mr. Ryan's not even in his grave yet."

"Steve," Edith admonished me. "It's not quite a receiving line. That'll be after the ceremony. He probably just happened to be standing there. The Greeks do tend to be clannish, you know, as so many cultures are. Probably a long-time friend of Aphrodite's."

She leaned close to me. "That's the daughter, over there by herself," she said in a low voice.

Mary Elizabeth was about fifteen, with a hunched posture that very clearly said "Don't talk to me." Her dark hair hung in ringlets around her head.

Edith and I chose not to follow the family to the cemetery, and instead I drove her home. And that was the last I thought of the Ryan family until I met Rick at his house to give our dogs a chance to play together.

We stood inside Rick's living room, watching Rochester romp around the back yard with Rick's Australian shepherd, Rascal. "Did you know Diana Ryan at school?" Rick asked.

"Sure. She lived across the lake from us. I just went to her father's funeral two weeks ago."

"And now her mother's dead," Rick said. "The ME said it was a heart attack, just like Mr. Ryan, and he was suspicious enough to do a full toxicological rundown. Turned up a high concentration of a chemical called aconite in her blood, which likely triggered the fatal attack."

"Wow. What kind of a chemical is aconite? A poison?"

Rick nodded. "According to the medical examiner, it's one of the oldest known poisons. Distilled from the roots of the buttercup plant. And it doesn't occur in any ordinary medications, though it does show up in small doses in some vitamin supplements. We have an order now to exhume Mr. Ryan's remains and see if the same conditions exist."

He took a sip from the bottle of beer he was holding, and I remembered Edith's comment about how low-class beer was back in the day. Now we were drinking Dogfish Head Ale, produced by a small-batch brewery in Delaware. Was that a sign of how far we'd come? Or of something else entirely?

"The Ryans seemed like such ordinary people," I said. "Who'd think someone would murder them."

"You know the main motives for murder as well as I do."

"Love, lust, lucre and loathing," I said.

"In a case like this, we look at *cui bono* – who benefits. Diana and her brother Clifford inherit their family money, so they're obvious suspects."

"Is there that much?"

"You know what a house like the Ryans' goes for in the Lakes these days? Even if it hasn't been fixed up, we're talking over a half-million bucks. Add in retirement accounts and savings, and even an ordinary couple can leave behind a substantial fortune."

"Do either Diana or Clifford have money problems?"

The dogs must have gotten tired or cold, because they rushed up to the door and barked to be let into the house. "That's up for investigation," Rick said. "The DA is putting together a subpoena for the whole family's finances."

Rochester and I went home soon after, but I was curious to see what I could find through legitimate means about the Ryan family. It was nosy, but in the past I'd been able to dig up information Rick could use. He had some online skills, but he was also burdened with antiquated systems and a lack of time. And I had some specialized knowledge I'd gained in my illegal exploits.

I had promised Rick that I'd abstain from any illegal activities online, and for the most part I'd been able to keep that promise. I began at Facebook, where I learned that Diana taught history and classics at Cambridge Academy. She had a quote from a poem by Linda Pastan: "I have become the very legend of fidelity."

I was curious to see what that meant, and discovered it was from a sequence of poems called "Rereading the Odyssey in Middle Age." The poem was in the voice of Argos, the loyal dog of Odysseus who waited twenty years for his master's return. Then, upon recognizing his scent, he died.

Not the most cheerful quote for a dog lover.

She had a master's degree in Classics and Ancient Mediterranean Studies from Penn State. A few pictures of her family—her husband, daughter, and her mother, though none with her father, and I remembered Edith saying that Diana and her father had been estranged. There were also lots of snapshots of Sophie, who was a couple of years older than Rochester.

I sent Diana a message with my condolences, and asked her to let me know if there was anything I could do. I got a return message soon after. "I haven't been able to take Sophie out much. Could you bring Rochester over sometime? We have a big yard where they can play."

I agreed and we made a plan for the next evening. It was still light after dinner as I followed the directions my phone app gave me and parked in front of a split-level house that badly needed a paint job. The landscaping hadn't been trimmed in ages, either, and the shriveled stump of a dead tree had pride of place in the front yard.

As Rochester and I approached, I heard arguing coming from the back yard, a man and a woman raising their voices. "Mary Beth needs braces," the woman said. "And this dentist is the only one who's capable of working with kids like her."

"I don't care," the man said. "We'd have to take out a second mortgage on the house to pay what he's asking. She'll have to wait until we see what we get from your parents' estate."

I stepped up to the door and rang the bell. After what seemed like a long time, the sullen girl I'd seen at the funeral answered the door. "What?" she asked.

Sophie the golden nosed past her and yipped at Rochester, and I let go of his leash so he could chase her into the house. "Rochester came for a play date," I said to the girl. I held out my hand. "Hi, I'm Steve."

She shrugged and turned away, leaving me to close the front door behind me and follow the dogs into the living room, where I could see Diana and her husband through the sliding glass doors, still arguing in the back yard.

The dogs rushed up to the doors and barked, and Diana saw me and waved. She came inside, and we hugged hello again. She brought out a platter of heart-shaped shortbread cookies mounded with powdered sugar, and we sat in the living room as the dogs romped around.

"These are delicious," I said, as the licorice tang in the shortbread mixed with the powdered sugar in my mouth, creating an explosion of flavor.

"They're called *kourabiedes*," Diana said. "They were my mother's specialty, though I can't make them nearly as well as she did. She used to get at least an inch of sugar to stand up on top."

Sophie rolled on her back and jiggled all four legs in the air as Rochester sniffed her. "Thanks for bringing Rochester over," Diana said. She wore a form-fitting white T-shirt with the cover image of Homer's *Odyssey* on it, and the legend "What a Trip!"

"I like your T-shirt," I said. "I took a seminar on the epic tradition in literature in college. *The Iliad*, *The Odyssey*, all the way up to Joyce's *Ulysses*. Though I had to read the Joyce twice to make sense of it."

"I love Homer," Diana said. "Maybe it's my Greek background, but he speaks to me. I teach it every year at the Cambridge School. It's a slog sometimes, but once you get students into the rhythm of it they start to appreciate it."

She stood up. "I have something else for you to try." She went into the kitchen and returned with a bottle of homemade ouzo and poured tiny cups for us.

I sipped it, then followed it with a cookie. "I can taste the licorice in these cookies even more after a hit of the ouzo."

"The ancient Greeks called ouzo the nectar of the gods," she said. "This comes from my mother's friend Nick. He makes it himself."

She sat back against the sofa. "I feel sorry for him. His wife died last year, and he moved back to Trenton, where he and my mother both grew up. They even dated when they were teenagers, and he was so pleased to reconnect with an old friend. Now she's gone, too."

"This ouzo doesn't have buttercup roots in it, does it?" I asked, only half joking.

"Buttercup roots? What an odd question. What makes you say that?"

Was Diana's defensiveness a sign that she knew how her parents had been poisoned? Rick must have spoken to her about the aconite when he sought to have her father exhumed.

Fortunately we were interrupted by loud music coming from upstairs, and Diana grimaced. "Sorry, that's Mary Beth. She's into this electronic music these days. I think she enjoys it because there are no words, and she can focus on the sounds. You know she's autistic?"

"Edith Passis mentioned it. It must be tough for you."

"It's a challenge, that's for sure. The only one who could really get through to her was my mother—all those years of teaching, I guess, added to the fact that she only had to deal with Mary Beth in small doses. Without her, I don't know what I'm going to do."

"I'm so sorry," I said. "My mom passed away quickly, too,

while I was living in California, so I never got to say goodbye to her properly." I shrugged. "My father, either." I was tempted to explain that I hadn't even been able to attend his funeral because I was in prison, but I resisted. I didn't know Diana that well, after all, and didn't need to burden her with my problems. "At least your mom had a good relationship with Mary Beth."

"Until last year." Diana took another gulp of the ouzo. "Then Mary Beth and my father got into a huge fight and she was banned from going over there. Fortunately my dad got over it just before he died, and Mary Beth was one of the last people to see him."

Mary Beth, who was fascinated by chemistry. Who had a difficult relationship with her grandfather, who might have known about aconite from her mother's interest in the ancient Greeks.

I had to get hold of myself. I was there to let Rochester play with Sophie, not to fabricate elaborate theories about who had poisoned the Ryans.

Sophie had gotten tired of playing by then, and Rochester came over to nuzzle me. The loud music was starting to give me a headache, so I made my excuses and my dog and I left.

I was troubled by what I'd heard at Diana's house, though, so on my way home I detoured past Rick's. By then, Rochester was ready to play again, and as he and Rascal romped, I sat in Rick's kitchen with a big glass of ice water and told him what I'd heard.

"I don't know if needing braces for their daughter qualifies as money problems, but Diana and George were arguing in the back yard when I got there."

"They wouldn't be able to get a second mortgage anyway," Rick said. "I did some searching online and found the property values in their neighborhood are tanking, and they're underwater on their first."

"Usually you leave the online stuff to me," I said.

"I have some skills, you know," he said. "What else did you

hear?"

I explained about Mary Beth and her autism. "I don't know if she can get violent, but she's certainly an angry girl, and Diana said she was one of the last people to see her grandfather alive. And apparently she's a chemistry whiz. Do you think that means she could have cooked up some buttercup roots and fed them to her grandfather?"

"Sounds a bit far-fetched, but you never know," Rick said.

"And Diana's a big fan of Greek literature," I said. "She probably knows about how aconite poisoning was used in history."

Rick wrote that information in the small notebook he carried with him. He'd done some investigating of Diana's brother Clifford, and he wasn't in any financial trouble, and by all accounts had a good relationship with his parents.

I left Rick's and drove home. I realized I hadn't mentioned the homemade ouzo to Rick, but Aphrodite's friend Nick had little connection to the family. I'd already spent too much time thinking about suspects, and I felt bad for Nick—I knew what it was like to lose a relationship, and it was a shame that his second try hadn't worked out.

The next day, as I poured Rochester's chow into a big plastic bowl and spritzed it with the glucosamine, I remembered what Diana had said about the ouzo. "Here you go, puppy," I said. "Nectar of the dogs."

He didn't seem to care – he wolfed the food down no matter what I did to it.

I was relaxing on the sofa a short while later when Edith Passis called me. "I'm so glad I got hold of you," she said, her voice quavering. "I'm not sure what I should do."

I sat up. Edith's health had been iffy for a while, including a broken hip, and I was worried. "What's the matter?"

"It's Diana Ryan. She's across the street starting to move some things out of her parents' house, and that man we saw at the funeral is there, too, and they're arguing. Should I call the police?"

"Does it look like he's trying to hurt her?"

"I don't know. But I'm so worried."

"I'll come over right now," I said. "If there's a problem I'll call Rick."

I piled Rochester into the car and we drove quickly to the Lakes. As I pulled up in front of Edith's house, I saw Diana and her husband George in front of a rental moving van. Nick, the man from the funeral, was there with them, and all three of them were yelling at each other.

"I'm telling you, you're not getting into this house," George said. "There's no reason why you need any kind of souvenir of my mother-in-law. You hardly knew her."

"She was the love of my life!" Nick insisted. "You don't know what we had between us."

I got out of the car and stood on the driver's side, with the car between me and the argument.

"My father was the love of my mother's life," Diana said. "Not you."

"At least let me have back the bottle of ouzo I gave her," Nick said. "That was a special blend I made just for her."

Rochester nuzzled me through the open window of the car, and I remembered the ouzo I'd shared with Diana. I hoped it wasn't from the same batch Nick had made for Aphrodite.

"No is no," George said. "You need to get out of here right now, or I'm calling the cops."

I made the call for George myself. "Rick?" I said, when he answered. "I'm at the Ryans' house and I think I know who poisoned Frank and Aphrodite."

While I was on the phone and not paying attention to him, Rochester scrambled out the window and took off for the Ryans' driveway. "Rochester!" I yelled. "Rick, I've got to go."

"I'll be right there. Don't do anything stupid."

I hung up the phone and rushed across the street, to where Rochester was jumping up on Nick. "Sorry, he got away from me," I said to Diana and George, as I struggled to get Rochester's leash on him.

"Nick was just leaving anyway," George said.

"I think he ought to stick around for a few minutes," I said. "I want to ask him about the ouzo he makes." I turned to the older man, who was still pushing Rochester away from him. "You must have a special recipe. "

"It's an old family one," Nick said. "Can you get this dog to leave me alone?"

"You doctor it up, don't you? With what? Buttercup roots?"

He looked at me, and I could see in his face that he knew what I was talking about.

"Buttercup roots?" Diana asked. "That's why you were asking about them the other day. What does that have to do with anything?"

Nick turned and tried to run away, but Rochester grabbed hold of his pant leg and wouldn't let go. "Aconite poisoning," I said. "You can distill the aconite from the roots of the buttercup plant."

Diana turned to Nick. "You poisoned my parents?" she screamed. "What kind of monster are you?"

She lunged at Nick and started to pummel him. George and I looked on, neither of us trying to stop her, and between her fists and Rochester's jaws, Nick wasn't going anywhere.

Rick's truck pulled up and he jumped out. "What's going on?"

"There's a bottle of Nick's homemade ouzo inside," I said. "I think you'll find it's the source of the aconite that poisoned Mr. and Mrs. Ryan."

It took some doing, but Rick got Diana to stop beating on

Nick, and Rochester to let go of Nick's pant leg. Rick handcuffed Nick and told him he was under arrest for suspicion of murder. He called the crime scene team to come over and search for the bottle of ouzo and take it into evidence.

Diana was crying in her husband's embrace. "I thought he was such a nice man," she said, as Rick led Nick away. "He had a sweet story about losing his wife and coming home."

"I wouldn't be surprised if he poisoned his wife the same way," I said. "But I don't get why he'd kill your mother if he was in love with her."

"She told me he was very pushy and she shoved him away." She looked up at me with her face tear-stained. "Do you think that if she'd only let him keep coming to see her she'd still be alive?"

"That's one of those questions nobody can answer," I said. "I doubt that even the oracle the ancient Greeks consulted could."

As I drove Rochester home, I thought about the ouzo Nick had prepared specially for Aphrodite and Frank Ryan. Nectar of the gods, indeed. For now, it was up to the judicial system to punish Nick—his judgment from the gods would come later.

Story 7: Dog's Only Son

I often say that my dog is the reason I get up every morning. Early, *every* morning. Rochester doesn't care what the time is; he's accustomed to the rising sun. On the first day after the change from daylight savings time he woke me shortly after sunrise. The clocks adjusted automatically, so they read about 6:45. But we'd gone to bed at our regular time the night before, so for me it was an hour earlier than normal.

All my golden retriever knew was that the sun was up, and that meant it was time for a walk.

I groaned and grumbled as Lili turned over and went back to sleep. I stumbled into a pair of sweatpants, a long-sleeved sweatshirt and fleece vest. I tucked a couple of plastic bags and my keys into one of the zippered pockets, grabbed Rochester's leash, and we were off.

The thirty-eight degree temperature hit me like a slap in the face as I opened the front door. It didn't seem to bother Rochester; he has a two-layer fur coat, with air pockets in between to keep him cool in summer and warm in winter.

He trotted down our street, Sarajevo Court, and the slanted roofs, bulbous dormers and double-paned windows of the Eastern European style matched the climate. I could imagine my great-grandparents emerging from old-style houses like these, though without central heating. And they'd be off to milk cows rather than walk a spoiled dog.

Rochester stopped periodically to sniff and pee as we made our way toward Ferry Street, which runs along one side of our gated community, River Bend, on its way to the long-gone ferry crossing on the Delaware River.

Fortunately, Rochester did his business a block before the guard house, and I picked it up, welcoming the warmth through the thin layer of plastic grocery bag. I immediately tugged him toward one of the doggie waste receptacles along River Bend Way, the community's main street.

These are circular green metal cans the size of a small wastebasket, with flap-down metal lid, and a dispenser of small waste bags beneath it. I opened the lid, as usual, and was about to drop the poop inside when I saw a tiny baby staring back at me.

"*Oy gevalt*," I said, in the language my people had used for generations at something that surprised them. I dropped the bag of poop to the ground and let go of Rochester's leash. I told him to sit, and he did, staring upward expectantly at the trash can.

I reached down into the can with my gloved hands and lifted out a baby who couldn't have been more than a few days old. He was wrapped in a soft blue blanket decorated with building blocks, and when I held his face up to my head he was cold to the touch. I quickly bundled him into my vest, close to my chest, and zipped the vest.

The blanket was thin and torn at one corner, certainly not enough to keep him warm on such a cold day. "Who could do something like this?" I asked Rochester, as I bent down and grabbed his leash. "You can drop a baby off at a firehouse or a police station, no questions asked. Who'd throw away a child?"

He didn't answer, but tugged me forward to the guard gate along River Bend Way. I had a complicated history when it came to offspring. My ex-wife had miscarried twice while we were married, and I felt the loss of those two little ones almost as much as she did. The miscarriages caused us both to do things we shouldn't have, and that led to our divorce.

I moved awkwardly, holding the leash with one hand and cradling the other over the baby. As I reached the gate house, the guard was inside behind a glass door, talking on the phone.

"Call 911!" I yelled. "Emergency!" I opened the zipper a bit to show him the baby inside my vest, and he ended his call and opened the sliding door to let me into the warm room. Rochester crowded in behind me and sat in the corner, his eyes on me.

When the guard reached the emergency operator, he handed the phone to me. "I need an ambulance immediately," I said. "The guard house to River Bend, right off Ferry Street in Stewart's Crossing. I found a baby in a trash can and he's still breathing, but he's very cold."

"What's the street address?" the operator asked.

I had no idea. "One thousand one River Bend Way," the guard said.

"And that's in what town?"

"Stewart's Crossing, Bucks County, Pennsylvania. Zip code 19066. Now can you please send an ambulance right away?"

"Service is on the way," she said, and I handed the phone back to the guard.

"Where did you find this little one?" the guard asked. He was a Hispanic guy in his early twenties with slicked-back dark hair and a face spangled with acne scars. He looked down at the baby and grabbed a woolen hat that was way too big, but he snuggled it over the boy's bald head.

"The green can about a block farther in from here," I said, and I started shivering. It wasn't the cold; the tiny booth was overheated. It was realizing that if we'd slept in that morning, or Rochester had pooped in a different area, we might never have found this infant and he might have died from the cold.

I stood back against the wall as the guard checked IDs for a couple of cars. I wondered idly who was coming to visit someone at River Bend at seven-something on a Sunday morning, especially one where the clocks had been turned back.

Then I came to the question I should have been asking all along. Where did this baby come from? One of my neighbors?

The ambulance came zooming in from Ferry Street, and I hurried outside to flag it into the single parking spot in front of the guard house. A young female EMT jumped out of the ambulance. "You reported a baby?"

I opened my vest and handed the baby to the young woman. He was warmer by then, and sneezed once. "He's adorable." She clambered into the back of the ambulance with the baby, and the driver came over to speak with me.

"Your baby?" he asked.

I shook my head. "I found him in a trash can." Now that I'd handed the boy over to someone who could help him, I was able to let go of the fear and emotion I'd held inside, and I started to cry. "Who would do such a thing?"

"It's good that you found him. I'm going to need your information to pass on to the police."

"Sure," I said. Rochester licked my hand as I gave the EMT my name, address and phone number. Then the girl called and told him they needed to get moving, and he jumped in and drove away.

I felt strangely unsettled as I walked back to Sarajevo Way. I'd done something good that morning, I knew. But the horror of the circumstances made me feel terrible.

When I got back to the house, I poured some kibble into Rochester's bowl and climbed the stairs, desperate to share my pain with Lili. She was still asleep, though, so I did the next best thing. I stripped down and slid under the covers, cuddling her, and let sleep take me away from my unhappiness.

We both woke around ten, and I told Lili what had happened, and she pulled me close and let me rest my head against her chest. "Oh, Steve," she said. "But the baby was all right when you handed him off to the ambulance?"

"He was. Later on I'll call the hospital and check on him."

Around noon, Rick Stemper called me. "Thanks for pulling me in to work on a Sunday," he said. "At least this is a change. Instead of a dead body you found a living one."

"In a trash can," I said, and once again I started to shiver with the import of the morning's activities.

"I'm on my way over," he said.

He brought Rascal, his Australian shepherd, and while Rochester and his friend romped around the house, tearing up and down the staircase and wrestling with each other, Rick and I sat at my kitchen table with cups of hot tea and I told him exactly what had happened that morning.

"You didn't see anyone nearby?"

I shook my head. "You think the mother was watching to see if someone picked up the baby?"

"No idea. Just covering all the bases."

"You could do a house-to-house survey in River Bend to see if any women were pregnant," I suggested.

"How many houses and townhouses in your community?"

"About seven hundred fifty."

"Let's see. Ten minutes at each house, that's what, a hundred twenty five man hours? Add in people who are out and have to be rechecked, that's what, about a month of my time?"

"You can't just let it go," I said.

"I'm not going to. I'll be making inquiries. Local women's health clinics, the high schools in case the mother is a teen."

It didn't seem like enough, but I understood Rick's dilemma. Yes, a crime had been committed. But the important thing was that the baby was in good hands.

"What will happen if you find the mother?"

"In Pennsylvania, child abandonment is a first degree

misdemeanor. If the mother—assuming that's who left the baby—is found guilty, she can serve up to five years in prison and pay a $10,000 fine." He shook his head. "All she had to do was drop the baby at a recognized location, no questions asked."

"What happens to the baby now?"

"If we can find a family member, he'll go there. If not, into the foster care system. Generally speaking, he'd be available for adoption in a year, if no family member surfaces."

He looked at me. "You're not considering adopting this baby, are you?"

I realized I'd never even considered that, and I shook my head. "I'm too old to be a first time dad. I just want what's best for him. Do you know how he's doing?"

"Apparently very well," he said. "I spoke to a nurse at the hospital before I came over here. He's very lucky you found him when you did."

"I hope that luck carries him forward," I said.

I was restless that afternoon and finally gave in and took Rochester for a long walk. It had warmed up by then, and he was eager to pull me along River Bend Way, not even stopping at the trash can where we'd found the baby. Instead, he kept going out to Ferry Road.

The gates at the entrance to River Bend served to control vehicular traffic into the community, but we were surrounded on two sides by a nature preserve, and there was an erratic pattern of fences and hedges along Ferry Road. Rochester wanted to turn right, toward the river, but staying inside the boundaries of our community.

I didn't know what he was looking for, but my golden retriever has a nose for crime, so I gave him his head and enjoyed the crisp, sunny Sunday afternoon as much as I could.

Suddenly he stopped along a section of dark green cypress, with sticky, aromatic branches. I noticed a shred of fabric in one of the branches, and realized that it matched the blanket the baby boy had been wrapped in.

I pulled out my phone, my hands shivering once again, and called Rick.

It was chilly standing there waiting for him and a crime scene tech, so Rochester and I patrolled the hedge, looking for any other evidence. By the time Rick arrived I was pretty sure that whoever brought the baby to River Bend had come in through that place in the hedge.

The tech, a young blonde in her late twenties, took photos and clipped the branch, sliding it into a paper evidence bag. "Did you lift any prints or DNA from the baby's skin or the blanket?" I asked Rick as we watched.

"No prints. Whoever handled the baby wore gloves, like you did. I sent the blanket off to be tested but I doubt we'll get much. If we find a woman we believe is the mother, we can do a DNA test, but there's nothing to do without someone to compare the baby to."

Once again, it felt like we were at a standstill. I had an idea that someone had brought this newborn into River Bend through the cypress hedge early on Sunday morning, but nothing more than that.

When I got back to the house, Lili was at her laptop at the kitchen table. "I'm asking people on Hi Neighbor if they know anyone in the area who was about to deliver," she said.

Hi Neighbor was a website for sharing neighborhood information, and you had to register with a street address within the parameters the site established. That meant not just River Bend, but some of the neighborhoods around us. "That's good, because I don't think the mother lived here." I told her what we had found.

"I wonder something." She went back to Hi Neighbor and did a couple of quick searches, then turned the computer toward me.

"There are cameras on all four sides of the guard house. Did you know that?"

"I didn't. You think one of them might have caught something?"

"Worth checking, don't you think?"

I looked at the phone. I could call Rick, but it was Sunday evening and I'd already dragged him out to River Bend twice that day. I decided to let him rest.

Monday morning, I took Rochester for his walk, and he decided he wanted to head across River Bend Way toward Minsk Court, where the community's clubhouse was. Of course it was closed that early in the morning, but he planted the idea in my head.

I set my own hours at Friar Lake, so at nine o'clock I called Joey Capodilupo and told him I'd be late. Then I walked over to the clubhouse, where I knew the association manager's secretary, Lois. She was a white-haired woman in her sixties, with red-framed glasses and a matching red beret, and her desk was cluttered with various mementoes of trips to Paris, including several miniature Eiffel Towers and colorful magnets from famous department stores.

I explained what I wanted to do. "I'll have to check with the manager," she said. "She's at a corporate meeting, though and I don't think I can reach her for a few hours."

"I'll be finished long before then," I said. "Please? Think about that little baby, abandoned in a trash can."

"All right. I'll set you up."

She led me into the manager's office and opened an app that let me view the security footage from the cameras on the guard house. It took a few minutes to figure out which camera I wanted, and then to scroll backwards to Sunday morning. Then I hunched over and watched a half-hour's worth of footage looking toward the cypress hedge.

Then suddenly there was movement, and a heavyset young woman in a knee-length down coat pushed her way through the hedge, carrying a bundle. The resolution wasn't good enough to see exactly what she was carrying, but I watched as the bundle caught on one of the cypress branches and she had to tug it loose.

She trudged forward, and as she got close to the guard house, though off to the right, I got a good look at her face.

I recognized her, but I wasn't sure from where. Didn't matter; I called Rick and asked him to meet me at the clubhouse.

As I waited, I kept staring at her. She was moon-faced, with a white ball cap that covered her hair. When Rick arrived, I showed him the footage, and Lois agreed, in her capacity as the association's representative, to make a copy of the tape for him.

Then I picked up Rochester and went to work. All day, the young woman's face haunted me, and Rochester was anxious as well. Finally late in the afternoon I sat down on the floor beside him and rubbed his belly. "What's the matter, puppy? Are you feeling sick? Do you want to go to Dr. Bob?"

Dr. Bob ran a small veterinary practice a few blocks down Ferry Road from River Bend, and Rochester usually didn't like to go there. The doctor and his staff were very kind and gentle, but still, there's something undignified about a stranger poking up your butt.

Surprisingly, as soon as I said Dr. Bob, Rochester jumped up happily.

That's when I knew what he was trying to tell me. I called Rick immediately. "I recognize that girl," I said. "She's a tech at the vet's office across from River Bend."

"Dr. Bob's office? I haven't been there in a while, but Rascal's due for his annual visit soon."

He blew out a short breath. "Guess I'll head over there now."

Lili and I had just finished dinner when Rochester began barking madly. "I know that bark," I said. "I'll bet it's Rick."

Sure enough, when I looked outside I saw Rick's truck pulling up in front of the house. "How does he do that?" Lili asked. "You think the truck makes a particular sound?"

"He's a detective dog. He knows things."

When Rick came inside, he confirmed what I had discovered. The young woman, whose name was Barbara Diaz, worked at Dr. Bob's office. Because she was heavy, she was able to conceal her pregnancy from her co-workers and her family. She had started experiencing labor pains Saturday night and had driven herself to Dr. Bob's office to look for pain pills, and given birth there. She had cleaned up the office then trudged over to River Bend, where she felt someone would discover the baby and take care of him.

Then she had gone home, and she was back at work on Monday, though Rick said she didn't look well at all. He had called an ambulance for her, and had an officer stationed at the hospital to put her under arrest as soon as she was well enough.

"And the baby?"

"She says she didn't know she could drop him off at a police station," Rick said. "I spoke to the district attorney, and he said that if Barbara will put the baby up for adoption immediately he'll consider reducing the charges against her."

Rochester sat up beside me and nuzzled my leg. "Rochester thinks that's a good idea," I said.

Story 8: Doggy DNA

As we walked down the alley behind the Chocolate Ear together, Rochester noticed the brindle boxer in front of the pawn shop at the corner of Ferry Street before I did. He's always eager to make new friends and thinks every dog on the street will be as gregarious as he is. Sadly, that's not always the case.

It was a gorgeous spring day, a cloudless blue sky above and the scent of lilac blossoms on the air. I planned to head to Ferry Street and take Rochester to the canal towpath for a long walk, but when I saw that boxer was alone, I tugged on Rochester's leash to turn around.

Rochester strained forward as the boxer lifted his leg on a stone planter of yellow daffodils in front of the pawn shop. Then the door swung open and a young woman rushed out. She had big round-framed sunglasses and a frizzy mop of bright red hair that immediately attracted my attention, and she wore a shapeless brown tent dress that swirled as she moved.

She took off toward Ferry Street, the boxer right behind her. As she ran, her head appeared to tilt to the right, and I realized as she grabbed at her hair that she was wearing a wig. I watched in fascination as she pulled the wig off. Then she and the dog turned the corner and were gone.

A moment later a portly man in baggy jeans and a fisherman's shirt came out of the pawn shop door. He looked up and down the alley. "You see a girl come running out of here?" he asked me, as Rochester and I approached.

"Yeah, with a bright red wig?" I asked. "She and her dog ran down to Ferry Street and turned right."

"She looked so innocent with that goofy red hair," he said. "I should never have turned my back on her."

"She stole something?"

"A diamond ring. Worth about five grand." He shook his head. "I'll have to call the cops and then the insurance company."

He went back inside grumbling. Rochester and I continued down the alley to Ferry Street. I tried to turn him toward the canal, but instead he pulled as if he wanted to cross the street.

"What is it, boy?"

I looked across the street in the direction he wanted to go. A young woman, of about the same shape and size of the pawn shop thief, was hurrying down the block, accompanied by a brindle boxer.

The same woman? This one had mousy brown hair cut short, and wore a bright yellow blouse and dark green shorts. She looked like a walking daffodil.

At first I thought it had to be a different woman and a different dog, but Rochester thought otherwise. The lack of a leash was the kicker for me.

We stayed on our side of the street and followed her up to Main Street. The boxer waited obediently by her side until the light changed. While we waited ourselves, I pulled out my cell phone and called Rick.

I told him about the girl and the dog, and he said, "I'm almost at the pawn shop. Keep an eye on her."

Rochester and I kept our distance as we followed the girl across Main Street and up a block, where she turned left. She climbed the porch of an old Victorian with fading paint on the green and white gingerbread.

She and the dog went inside, and Rochester and I waited in the shade of a big maple just coming into leaf until Rick arrived a few minutes later, parking his unmarked car on the side street.

"You sure it's the same girl?" he asked, as he reached down to chuck Rochester under his chin.

"Can't say. Same body type, and it's definitely the same dog. Rochester recognized him."

"Huh. The crime dog strikes again."

Despite his skepticism, I knew that Rochester and I had converted Rick into a believer in my dog's detective abilities.

"All the pawn shop guy remembers is the bright red hair," he said. "He couldn't identify her."

"What about the dog?"

"He didn't say anything about a dog."

"Rochester and I saw the dog, a brindle boxer, pee on the planter in front of the pawn shop. I'll bet you could get the dog's DNA and match it. They do that kind of thing now, you know."

"Not in Stewart's Crossing," he said. "The chief would laugh me right out of his office if I suggested that."

"But the girl doesn't have to know that. You're always complaining that people assume too much from DNA evidence, right? That they have no idea how complicated it is?"

"Yeah."

"So when you talk to her, tell her that you got the dog's DNA from the planter, and if she wasn't with him, then someone else was, and you need to take the dog in for evidence."

He shook his head, and I wasn't sure he was going to take my idea. He was the cop, after all. My dog and I were just amateurs.

Rochester and I went for a long walk along the canal towpath, enjoying the spring weather, and it wasn't until dinner time when Rick called. "Never underestimate the dumbness of the common criminal," he said. "She bought the story about the doggie DNA. She said she'd hand over the diamond ring if I didn't take her dog away. "

"Lesson learned. Next time you're going to commit a crime, leave the dog at home."

Rochester woofed in agreement.

Story 9: Walking the Dog: A Story in Text Messages

I'm always interested in trying new techniques and fictional forms, and I read recently about a website that publishes very short stories composed only of text messages. I wrote this, and though it's not really reflective of the golden retriever mysteries (Rochester would never do this!) I thought it was fun and wanted to share it with you.

Steve: Gross. Rochester just threw up

Lili: What do you want me to do? Clean it up!

Steve: I can't, there's something in the vomit

Lili: Animal vegetable or mineral?

Steve: Animal

Steve: Looks human

Steve: Like a finger

Lili: A HUMAN FINGER!

Steve: With nail polish

Lili: The dog bit someone's finger?

Steve: I think he ate it while we were walking

Lili: That dog gets into more trouble than a bunch of monkeys on crack

Steve: Oh shit.

Lili: What?

Steve: You know how Maria next door likes to paint stars on her nails?

Lili: The dog ate our neighbor?

Steve: So far just the finger. I'll take him out to poop again.

Thanks for reading! I'd love to stay in touch with you. Stop by my website any time, and subscribe to one or more of my newsletters: Gay Mystery and Romance or Golden Retriever Mysteries. I promise I won't spam you!

I hope you've liked reading these stories about the adventures Steve and Rochester get into between books. It has been fun for me to write them, incorporating bits and pieces of my childhood and the people and places I grew up with.

If you liked this book, please consider posting a brief review—seriously, Amazon only requires a minimum of twenty words! Reviews at Amazon, Goodreads and in reader groups help other readers discover books they'd want to try.

You can also follow me at Goodreads to see what I'm reading, and my author page at Facebook where I post news and giveaways.

WEBSITE:
   www.goldenretrievermysteries.com

BLOG:
   http://mahubooks.blogspot.com

AMAZON AUTHOR PAGE:
   http://www.amazon.com/-/e/B001JP4EL6

FACEBOOK:
   https://www.facebook.com/neil.plakcy

GOODREADS:
   http://www.goodreads.com/author/show/126217.Neil_Plakcy

PINTEREST:
   http://pinterest.com/neilplakcy/boards/

TWITTER:
   https://twitter.com/NeilPlakcy

The Series in Order

In Dog We Trust

The Kingdom of Dog

Dog Helps Those

Dog Bless You

Whom Dog Hath Joined

Dog Have Mercy

Honest to Dog

Dog is in the Details

Dog Knows

Dog's Green Earth

If you're a Kindle Unlimited reader, you'll find omnibus volumes of books 1-3 (Three Dogs in a Row); books 4-6 (Three More Dogs in a Row); and books 7-9 (Another Three Dogs in a Row) there for you to enjoy.

About the Author

Neil Plakcy's golden retriever mysteries are inspired by his own golden, Samwise, who was just as sweet as Rochester, though not quite as smart. And fortunately he didn't have Rochester's talent for finding dead bodies. Now that Sam has gone on to his big, comfy bed in heaven, his place by Neil's side has been taken by Brody and Griffin, a pair of English Cream goldens with a penchant for mischief.

A native of Bucks County, PA, where the golden retriever mysteries are set, Neil is a graduate of the University of Pennsylvania, Columbia University and Florida International University, where he received his MFA in creative writing. A professor of English at Broward College's South Campus, he has written and edited many other books; details can be found at his website, http://www.mahubooks.com. He is also past president of the Florida chapter of Mystery Writers of America.

www.ingramcontent.com/pod-product-compliance
Lightning Source LLC
LaVergne TN
LVHW012021060526
838201LV00061B/4406